Wolf

A PARANORMAL ROMANCE THAT BITES!

N GRAY

Print ISBN 978-1-991206-13-8
First Edition 2021
Previously published in the Once You Go Shifter Anthology
Second Edition June 2022
Published in South Africa by Cutman Press

Claire

This story contains content that might trouble some readers, including, but not limited to, depiction of and references to death, mental and physical abuse, sexual assault, violence, and murder.

Please be mindful of these and other triggers; practice self-care before, during, and after reading.

Today was going to be a great day—I could feel it. Everything was going to go my way. I'd woken on the right side of the bed. My makeup was just right, and my hair was behaving. I was ready to start my Friday with a spring in my step. My bosses had started a new case and said I could join them if I wanted to. But I'd first see how much admin still needed finishing before joining them.

My jeans slipped over my hips and butt without effort or needing to suck in my stomach; the latest exercise routine I'd started was working. I'd lost some weight, although I still had a few pounds to go. I'd gained some muscle and hadn't felt better in years. I never thought my late thirties were going to be this hard, and was dreading my forties, even though it was only three years away.

The only thing that could upset me today was the awfully long queue outside my favorite coffee shop. I grumbled to myself when I stood behind a man speaking to someone on his phone, writing down the list of coffee orders. This was going to take forever.

Unfortunately, I was as mundane as humans came and couldn't freeze the line, so I could cut in front. I'd have to wait like the rest of the sheeple for my delicious cappuccino.

There were other coffee shops in Sterling

Meadow, but this one I *loved*. Their coffees were smooth, rich, and mouth-watering. I only had one tiny addiction—coffee. I wasn't a connoisseur, per se, but I liked what I liked. And this coffee was the absolute best; *magnifique*, as the French would say.

The line moved, and I was finally inside the shop. Peering around the shoulders of the man in front of me, I glimpsed at the counter. I moaned inwardly and hoped the owner didn't see me. Not that I didn't like Jason; he was gorgeous to look at, but... there was always a *but*. He was a wolf. An alpha were-wolf part of Shawn's pack. And he owned the best freaking coffee in town. What alpha wolf, in his right mind, did that? A man like him should be out doing wolf stuff, not mess with my coffee, or bake the best muffins. Yet, it was his coffee I craved and bought daily.

"Claire!" boomed his voice from behind the counter. "Your order is ready."

If this was any other coffee shop, I'd gladly smile and head over to the front, passing all the waiting suckers. But this was Jason's coffee shop, and I'd hoped he wasn't in today. The moon was full last night, and his kind usually hunted all night and slept all day. But he wasn't sleeping. No, not this man. He had to be in his shop, staring right at me.

I didn't like him much. But I wanted my coffee more. I sucked up my ego, avoided eye contact with

3

the other patrons as I passed them, and headed for the counter.

I felt Jason's dark gaze rake over my body, and I wanted to squirm. When I glanced up, his smiling blue eyes penetrated mine, and I touched my clothing instinctively—I still had my clothing on and nobody else was watching me. It was only Jason's intense stare, making me feel this way.

Jason wasn't drop-dead-drool-all-over-yourself kind of gorgeous; he was ruggedly handsome. He had a slightly crooked nose, a scar on his chin which was hidden beneath his short brown beard, and one ear was slightly pointy at the top. I may have been staring at him for longer than necessary, but then again, he was staring back.

And he was a were-wolf.

I couldn't say for sure when I started hating were-wolves. I just did. They smelled like the earth, powerfully built, and most of them exuded dominant sex pheromones that tested my ovaries.

My core spasmed, and I shoved that feeling down and glowered at Jason when he approached the counter with a delectable smile.

"I didn't order yet," I said softly so only his super ears heard.

"After all these months you've been coming into my coffee shop, you'd think I wouldn't know your order by now?" he asked rhetorically, pushing the

takeaway cup and bag filled with two warm chocolate muffins that oozed chocolate bits my way. His
large, powerful hands lingered on my items. The
muscles on his tanned forearms bunched. I wondered
if he was testing me and whether I'd touch his hands
when I took my order from him.

My mouth watered. I wanted. Give me. Now! My
anger dissolved on my tongue, and I fished for the
money.

I flinched when an enormous hand touched mine.
My gaze travelled up his muscular forearm until I
reached his pleasantly smiling face.

"My treat," he said with a gruff, masculine voice.

"I don't want to owe you anything," I said and
slapped money on the counter. "Keep the change." I
grabbed my goodies and hurried out the door before
he stopped me.

There was something wrong with that man. I
didn't know why Jason did that to me, but he did,
and I hated it. I hated him. But after one sip of his
coffee, I practically melted onto the sidewalk. It was
orgasmic. And the chocolate muffin. Oh my gods,
better than sex.

My thoughts drifted to a dark bedroom with a
naked Jason, and I shook the vision away with a
shudder. That would never happen. Besides,
someone like him probably dated all the women in
town, and I didn't want to be just another notch on

his very long and very thick belt. Oh, gods... I didn't even want to go there.

Besides, I had a boyfriend. Which reminded me. I pulled out my cellphone and sent Erik a text message about our date tonight. It was our six-month anniversary, and I had a sneaky suspicion he was about to ask me to move in with him. I was so excited. Things were finally going well for me. Erik still gave me butterflies in my stomach when we touched. That had to mean something.

Erik was one of those silent, sensitive types, while I was slightly on the loud and wild side compared to him. And ever since I'd met him, I'd calmed down a little, because I wanted things to work out between us. Erik was a late bloomer, and I was the first person he'd ever slept with. I never made him feel embarrassed about that fact, ever. He was seven years my junior, but he was mature for his age.

I enjoyed the rest of my muffin, threw the empty liner in the trash can and pocketed the second muffin. I climbed the three steps and entered the building where I worked. Our office was on the fifth floor, but I hardly saw my bosses; Blaire and Ralph. Ulysses Assassins was a monster contract killer agency that became a legal entity when they started working with the police. I was a recent addition to the team because they were so busy, they needed someone to do their administration, legal paperwork, and even balance the books. Since I was a brainiac, although I never finished college, I taught myself how to do everything and I did it well. Blaire had even given me a bonus last month because I'd caught up with all their admin.

I reached my floor and came across Josh, the little five-year-old brat who belonged to the lawyer across the hallway. He was a busy-body but in hindsight a very sweet kid.

"What you got there?" he asked inquisitively, his big brown eyes staring at my bulging pocket.

"It's a surprise. Do you want to see it?"

He nodded so vigorously I thought his head was about to fly off.

"I got you a special muffin again today. Do you want it?" Yesterday I brought him a bran muffin, and it surprised me that Jason had packed two chocolate muffins today without me asking. I smiled at the thought, then frowned at his audacity. I should've appreciated it, but he was a were-animal, a were-wolf, and I hated them all.

Josh's smile split his face in two, and he held out his hands. The office door where his mom worked opened, and she stood in the doorjamb, her slender figure silhouetted by the light behind her.

"Josh! I hope you aren't pestering Claire, again?"

"It's fine, Lucy. Can I give him a muffin?"

"Thanks, Claire. You can," Lucy said, then her

voice changed to that commanding tone that made me want to do everything she asked. "Then you come back here, Josh. You know I don't like it when you wander around."

"Thank you, Miss Claire." Josh grabbed the muffin out of my hands and ran to his mother.

I unlocked and entered my office, set my half-empty cup on my desk, switched on my laptop, and sat behind my desk to start working.

Blaire had asked whether I wanted to work from home. Although I loved my home, my apartment was too small to live and work in the same space. I'd go insane, and she'd have to visit me at that special ward, providing care for those in dire need.

My inbox pinged with all the new emails, and I started my workday.

Claire

I finished work around five. On my way home, I had to pass Jason's coffee shop, which was aptly named *'Alpha Coffee'*. I snorted at the irony. The doors were already closed, and the lights were off. From what I knew, Jason kept it open till about three in the afternoon. What he did to fill the rest of his time, I didn't know. He was probably at his pack's clubhouse, or whatever they called it.

When I arrived home, I got ready for my date with Erik.

Erik had texted letting me know he was coming directly to the restaurant after work and asked that I meet him there.

I dressed in my stylish jeans, and wore a pretty blouse with a jacket over it. I managed to put on some makeup, making me feel ready to tackle the world.

At seven o'clock I entered our favorite Italian place and found our regular table at the back which Erik had reserved for our date. I ordered a couple of whiskeys for us and perused the menu while I waited for him.

After thirty minutes and two whiskeys later, Erik finally arrived, looking a bit disheveled.

"What happened to you?" I asked, staring at the buttons of his shirt. He'd gotten dressed in a hurry and buttoned the wrong holes. His hair was sticking up in all directions, and he quickly tucked in his shirt. "It looks like you fell off a truck or out of bed." I swallowed hard as I stared at his attire.

"Yeah, sorry about that," he said nervously, glancing over his shoulder.

I ignored the hollow feeling in my stomach and called the server over and ordered another round of drinks.

"I can't stay," he said, while remaining standing.

"What?" I yelled. "You just got here, and it's our anniversary," I said in a slightly softer tone so that the other patrons would stop staring.

"I know and I'm sorry." He glanced over his shoulder again. I peered around him. Outside in the distance, a woman stood beside a tree with her arms crossed over her chest, staring our way.

I leaned back in the chair and folded my arms. That sinking feeling became a raging inferno. And I wanted to jump over the table and rip his heart out. I blinked rapidly because I would not cry.

"I'm sorry—"

"Don't say you're sorry. Just spit it out." I croaked, not liking how desperate I sounded.

"It just happened." He exhaled and bowed his head. When he glanced up at me, his eyes glistened in the light. "I never wanted to hurt you. I'll tell you anything you want to know."

"Who is she?"

"She's a friend of a client. I first met her at a client's meeting, then we bumped into each other a couple of days ago and we went for coffee. It escalated pretty quickly after that."

The back of my throat ached as I tried to swallow. When I finally found my voice, I spoke. "So you chose today, our six-month anniversary, to tell me you're fucking another woman?" I yelled. Other patrons glanced nervously our way, then quickly at their food when I asked if they wanted something.

"Shh," he mumbled, embarrassed by my outburst. "I wanted to tell you on Wednesday already, but you were in such a good mood. And then yesterday came and went. Then today I realized I couldn't lie to you anymore. I thought nothing would happen between Mindy and me, but it did, and I really like her."

"You like her more than the person you've been sleeping with for six months. Is she so much better than what I've given you?" I said through gritted teeth.

"It's not like that, Claire. Don't compare yourself to her. You are very different. I know I'm the ass," he said, glancing around. "I've paid for your dinner already. Order whatever you want. And I'll send over the rest of your stuff from my apartment tomorrow," he said clinically, like he'd rehearsed his speech for days and no longer felt anything. That the last six months of us being together meant nothing to him. That I was disposable; kicked to the curb like garbage.

I couldn't answer him. Tears welled in my eyes, my heart cracked, and I'd lost my appetite.

"I'm sorry," Erik said, turning around and left without glancing at me.

I tried not to see where he was going, but I did. I watched him snake his arm around her waist like he used to around me, and I burst into tears.

And I thought my day would be great—it was one of the worst.

The server darted over, offering me napkins. He set the two whiskeys down and offered to take my order. He'd overheard my break-up and tried to console me. I swatted his hand away and told him to bring me the bottle of his finest whiskey and a seafood pasta dish. Erik was paying after all.

———

Three hours later, I stumbled out of the restaurant before they called the police. I may have thrown my empty plate at the manager, pushed over a table, and smashed a chair into the wall. I decided it was best for all if I left before Blaire needed to bail me out of jail.

Not wanting to go home to my dark, very empty, and depressing apartment. I crossed the street and headed for the park. I loved visiting parks as a kid, but as an adult I was way too busy. Erik never liked the outdoors, and I tried to do what he wanted.

"Ugh," I grumbled when I thought of Erik again. I was doing so well. The whiskey amnesia had almost worked. *Almost.* Until I thought of the park and the trees and how I wanted to go hiking, but Erik hated it. Then my thoughts swarmed around in my head of us in his apartment, then in mine. Then memories of us going to the movies or a restaurant surfaced. Our social life consisted mainly of visiting friends and doing mundane human things.

As much as I hated him and enjoyed doing those things. I didn't think I'd ever want to do them again.

I never wanted to watch a movie again, eat out, or visit friends. All I wanted to do was mope and wallow in my misery. Misery loved company.

I staggered through the dark alley toward the gate leading to the park, tripped over trash, and landed on my hands and knees. I burst out laughing at my silliness and that I hadn't been drunk like this in years.

Using the wall to steady myself, I meandered through the entrance and fell again, but this time on soft grass. My thoughts sobered. Tears pricked at my eyes. The silence of the park deafening.

Casting an eye around the enormous park, I didn't hear any night calls of animals or stridulation of insects; I was utterly alone. There was nothing but emptiness fueled by my loneliness. And I let go. I gave in to the sadness, and bawled until my throat was hoarse, my face swollen and most probably red, and my nose in desperate need of a blow. I hadn't ugly-cried in years, but tonight it was necessary.

I allowed myself the time to mourn the loss of a boyfriend I thought I'd loved. He was the first man I took a chance on after I told myself *never again*. I would use this time to get it out of my system. To get over Erik and to never think of him, or our time together, again. Not wanting to become a walking disaster, I knew I had to move on.

I wiped away the irritating tears with the back of

my hand, stood tall, raised my head, pushed my shoulders back and traversed farther into the play area. The smell of damp ground and freshly cut grass wafted in the air. But the dark shadows beyond the border left me wondering whether I'd made a mistake coming here.

There were still no animal or insect sounds, and the winds whispered through the trees, creating ominous sounds that caused my arms to pebble.

When my thoughts sobered me completely, I realized I was in the same park where they had attacked Blaire. This happened about four years ago and they had almost killed her; two different were-animals had left her for dead. I wondered whether it was safe for me to be here at this godly hour.

Swallowing my nervousness, I headed toward the exit. But the door was now closed. I was sure I'd just used that door when dread flooded my system. Now I stood with clarity. A chill ran down my spine. I felt another presence behind me; the weight of its stare unbearable.

A low, rumbling growl echoed around me. The hairs on my body stood on end. The thought of becoming a predator's dinner left a nasty taste in my mouth, and I spun around, coming face to face with a large-ass wolf. He snarled at me, baring his large canines. Its hungry gaze wanting to feast on me.

I didn't understand why, but the first thing that

popped into my head was the coffee shop. "Jason? Is that you?"

The were-wolf stepped closer, growled, and showed me his teeth and blood-soaked muzzle. His black coat glistened in the moonlight, and I thought I saw a red shine.

Swallowing my screams, I realized he'd been hunting, and I was next on his list.

I raised my arms to show I was unarmed and stepped backward. The wolf snapped its jaw and closed the distance. I didn't want to know how it felt between its jaws; I spun around and dashed toward the entrance on the other side of the park.

I didn't get far.

A heavy weight crashed on top of me and I kissed the dirt. My head smacked the sandy surface with a loud thud, the wolf's claws digging into my back as its enormous jaws clamped down on my shoulder. I screamed blue murder, hoping someone would assist.

Nobody arrived.

It bit down harder, it's huge teeth cutting more of my muscle and tissue. The pain seared through my back, burned through my veins, and tingled down to my toes.

I lay frozen, too scared to move in case it decided to rip its jaw from my body and took a large piece of me with it.

It was too dark and too late for anyone to venture out this side of the area, and I realized I needed to save myself. But in order to do that, I had to get this thing off me first or become human kibble.

"No!" I shrieked. With all my strength I turned over. The wolf unclenched its jaw from my shoulder and jumped off. But when I was on my back, it pounced on me again. He lay on top of me, pressing his large thing between my legs, and snapped its muzzle in my face. To protect myself, I raised my forearm, and he bit down. Hard.

For a moment my pulse raged in my ears, my heart thundered in my chest, and I closed my eyes. Tonight was one of the worst evenings, and to top it off, I was going to die. If I didn't do something, I would become this were-wolf's meal, and nobody would care that I was gone. My corpse would remain unclaimed and unnamed, and I'd have a pauper's burial. I was sure Blaire and Ralph would miss me and perhaps claim my body, but I'd only been working for them for five months. I didn't think they cared.

The surrounding air moved as the wind changed direction. Thoughts of strength flooded me and I knew I couldn't give up. This was an evening from Hell and I'd like a refund. One particular thought swirled around in my small brain; I couldn't give up. I couldn't let Erik, the asshole, ruin my life, and I couldn't allow this asshole-beast to get the best of me —or eat me.

The wolf pressed his thing harder against my core as he salivated over my arm. His sharp clawed paws stood on either side of my head, and I felt his hot, foul breath against my cheeks. With his large head close to mine, I saw his hungry gray-colored eyes with flecks of green.

When I moved my arm, he clamped down harder. Bursts of pain shot up my shoulder and I cried out again. Anger raged through my veins and another burst of adrenaline coursed through my system and on instinct I shoved two of my fingers into one of his eyes, gripped the squishy organ, and ripped it out.

The wolf yelped, letting go of my forearm, and moved away from me as it tried to assess its wound. I used the opportunity to ram my fist into its jaw. A loud snap sounded, and I kicked him in the balls. The wolf fell over, affording me the chance I desperately needed, and moved farther away from him. I cradled my injured arm against my chest and sprinted for the exit.

I glanced over my shoulder, but the big, bad wolf had disappeared. If it wasn't for the pain lacing my body, I would've thought I'd dreamed it all.

With adrenaline still coursing through my veins, I ran as fast as I could until I reached my apartment complex doors and entered the building.

Everything was a blur; running across the park toward my apartment block and entering my apartment. I couldn't recall how I got home. I was just grateful I arrived here without any other incident.

Once inside my apartment, I slammed the door shut, and dead bolted the locks. With my back against the door, I stood motionless. My body trembled until I could no longer stand, and I crashed to the floor in a heap of limp limbs and more tears.

I flinched when my shoulder touched the door, and I realized I should've gone to the emergency room. I couldn't leave now; the beast could be out there waiting for me. Not wanting to leave the safety of my apartment, I leaned on my good arm and stood with a grunt. My head swirled now that the adrenaline started tapering off. Every part of my body ached; my shoulder throbbed and burned while my forearm felt raw and exposed to the elements.

I glanced at myself in the bathroom mirror and recoiled. Mud caked my face and body where I'd fallen on my front and back. And the beast had torn chunks of flesh from my shoulder and forearm and had ripped my clothing. My bra was on its last thread, my makeup had smudged across my eyes and cheeks from crying, and my hair was knotty and messy. It amazed me nobody had seen me in this condition. But as I thought about it, I couldn't recall seeing anyone as I dashed through the streets.

Desperately wanting to clean myself of the wolf's saliva and scum, I undressed, wincing every step of the way. Slowly, I climbed into the shower. The scorching water splashed against my aching body. My shaking limbs eased as the warm water caressed every inch of me.

I allowed myself to cry in the quiet of my bathroom. This would be the last time, I promised myself. I wouldn't cry over Erik ever again. And I vowed to hunt down the beast who'd bitten me.

Claire

My dreams came in short, scary bursts of pain, blood, and tears. My mind crashed as the fever spiked, and I was sure I was dying. The clothing and bedding soaked with my body fluids, yet I didn't have the strength to get up and fetch a dry set.

Even though I said to myself while I showered that that was the last time I'd wallow in sadness. But right now, I couldn't bring myself to do anything. I wanted to die. I was ready to die. And I'd do so gladly.

My chest ached, and a tightness left me breathing short and shallow as I struggled to fill my lungs. I didn't bother cleaning the wounds with any antiseptic ointment because I knew I needed a tetanus shot or something lethal, and the way I felt it should just get infected and kill me already.

These self-destructing thoughts were not mine. Yet they swam around in my mind all night long; as if the owner of those words wanted to inflict more pain and despair. I wondered whether these thoughts were caused by the infected wound or the wolf who had bitten me. And had somehow infiltrated my mind.

One after the other, these thoughts crashed into me like a never-ending story, leaving me exhausted and cowering in pain.

When the bright sun crept through the curtain, blinding me, I shrank under the damp sheet. It was only the stench of my room that forced me out of bed.

Moving in slow motion and careful not to hurt myself further, I removed the damp bedding. I undressed and threw everything into the washing machine and showered again.

I needed to tend to my wounds before they festered. My head ached so badly it felt as though a jackhammer was drilling into my skull. My thermometer read one-oh-five. I knew that any temperature over 103 F required urgent care. I sighed knowingly. I needed help.

The wound on my shoulder now raised, an angry red with pus oozing out. The bite on my forearm didn't look as bad, but it was just as gross. I probably needed strong antibiotic injections and stitches, but too much time had passed. I glanced at my clock, which read it was already eleven in the morning. My phone had no messages because it was the weekend, therefore nobody needed me.

With no medical insurance or cash for the emergency room, my basic first aid kit would have to do. I removed my kit from under the bathroom counter and opened it. Noting two of my fingernails had torn, I grabbed the nail clippers and trimmed the jagged edges first.

I was sure Blaire would help me with some money, but I didn't want to bother her—yet. The last thing she needed was an employee disturbing her for cash. But that's just it—I knew she would go out of her way to help me. That's one reason I applied to work for her. I'd read about her story online, so I knew what she'd gone through. I also knew how the Master vampire of Sterling Meadow and a were-leopard had helped her through everything. I knew she'd help me, but I didn't think I was worth it.

Again, those dark, self-loathing thoughts filled my mind.

Admittedly, some of those thoughts were mine. Unfortunately, when one grew up the way I did, self-worth was a tricky subject. My parents had dumped me with a relative, and that relative had dumped me on a church step. The nun who had looked after us had kept the note and basket they had brought me in with, and when I was ready to leave; she gave it back to me. It basically told me my parents were useless teenagers and didn't know how to take care of a baby. There was no information on the useless relative, though. But they drove a red car as told by the nun.

Ever since then, I'd learned to rely on myself. I had tried relying on others, but they always disappointed me. So, I stopped expecting anything from anyone.

I exhaled a shaky breath as I came to terms that I might need help. If I didn't feel better by this evening, I'd call Blaire. She might know what to do or who I could go to for this kind of injury.

Thankful my wounds weren't gushing blood; I cleaned and bandaged the damaged areas as best I could and downed two painkillers. My body throbbed with a constant ache that left me wanting to scrape my skin off.

Satisfied the bandages wouldn't come off. I dressed, placed clean linen on the bed and climbed back in bed under the dry covers.

———

I awoke with a start. My stomach rumbled, and my mouth salivated. A hunger so great it physically pained. My stomach twisted and all I thought about was eating steaks, burgers, and beef tacos.

I climbed out of bed and inspected my kitchen for something to munch. I opened the fridge to find a three-day-old mince; I brought the opened container near my nose and gagged, throwing it away along with everything in my fridge that smelled funky. I left the carton of milk and condiments. I peeked inside my pantry, but all that revealed was how sad my shopping attempts were.

Groaning inwardly, as much as I didn't feel like doing anything today, I needed to buy groceries or fast food.

I grabbed the largest sweater I could find and pulled it on along with sweat pants. I slipped on my sneakers without socks and flinched at my reflection. My clothing hung on my emaciated frame; my face gaunt and skin pale. Dark circles surrounded my once bright blue eyes that now looked ghostly-gray. I didn't feel sexy at all and skipped adding any makeup, I didn't think it would help anyway. Instead, I grabbed a baseball cap and pulled it down as low as it could go.

The moment I closed the front door behind me,

my pulse thundered in my ears. As much as I'd prefer to stay inside where it was warm and safe, I needed food. My stomach growled again followed by an intense stabbing pain, there was no way I could ignore that hunger.

I glanced left and right for neighbors, but it was only me in the dark hall. The floor and walls swam when I took a step toward the stairs, and if I didn't lean against the wall, I would've crashed to the ground.

I managed to get to the staircase without falling and gripped the hand railing to keep steady. I traversed down the stairs slowly, swallowing hard with each step. The waves of nausea were about to bubble over if I didn't concentrate on the exit and the fact that I needed food.

Once I reached the exit, the noises outside my apartment building boomed in my ears. A car passing sounded like a jet engine. Birds tweeting sounded like shrieking inside my eardrums. The cool air blew hot against my skin leaving goosebumps. While the sun seared my eyeballs. I pulled out my sunglasses and slipped them on. Feeling my pocket, the cash from my drawer, still secure.

I loved where I lived; it was within walking distance to shops and to my work. I didn't drive, which made things tricky, but I had everything I needed right here.

Before I bought groceries, I headed for the coffee shop. My mouth watered just thinking about the delicious cup of hot java. Thinking about drinking coffee gave me the boost of energy I needed to walk the short distance without tripping over my feet.

The doors at *Alpha Coffee* were still open, with five minutes to spare. The shop was empty, apart from the barista behind the counter. I exhaled with relief.

"Good afternoon," she said with a broad smile, but the closer I got to her, her face dropped. I didn't know what her problem was, but I couldn't look that bad to warrant her expression. "Uh, can I get you something to drink?" she asked, averting her eyes.

"Please," I grumbled, sucked in a deep breath, and continued. "Can I have a cappuccino, please? And do you have any chocolate muffins left?"

"We do," she said quickly and headed toward the back.

I heard heavy footsteps heading toward the counter from the other side of the shop, and Jason entered with a broad smile. Then something flickered in his eyes, concern maybe, or annoyance; I didn't know which. And his expression shifted into one I'd never seen before—serious.

"Claire," he said, plastering on a smile. "Are you okay?"

"I'm fine. I just want my coffee," I grumbled,

swallowing hard, but the back of my throat felt like razor blades.

"Sure, I'll make your coffee while Mandy gets you one of my freshly baked muffins." He moved toward the large coffee maker that stood to one side. He kept stealing glances my way as he made my coffee.

I groaned under my breath, turning around so I didn't have to see him. The air inside the coffee shop felt hot and stuffy, and I aired out my oversized top.

I flinched when clanging of the cup echoed in my eardrum, forcing me to step backward to keep my balance. The closing of the oven door felt like a glass window crashed against the side of my head.

I sucked in a deep breath. Sweat beaded my forehead, which I wiped away with my sleeve.

Jason smashed the porta filter thingy against the side to empty the used ground coffee, and the sound reverberated inside my chest. I wanted to snarl at him for making such a noise, but I didn't want to attract unwanted attention.

When bile rose, I swallowed hard. I hurried toward the door and stood in the doorjamb for some fresh air. My breathing steadied as I sucked in air deeply until I filled my lungs and then exhaled. The air cooled my skin and was sure my temperature dropped a degree.

When a hand grabbed my shoulder, I recoiled, tripping over my feet, and fell to the ground.

"Christ, are you okay?" someone asked behind me, their voice dreamlike and at a distance.

Powerful hands grabbed me and lifted me off the sidewalk. The sudden movement disorientated me. I doubled over, dry-heaving until I could breathe again.

"What happened, Claire?" Jason asked, no longer sounding ghostly.

"I'm fine, it's just a cold... or something," I said, swatting his hands off me.

"That's not a cold," he stated matter-of-factly.

I wasn't in the mood for him chastising me and walked away, but his large hand curled around my bicep.

"At least take your coffee and muffin with you." His voice was deep and authoritative; I couldn't deny him.

"Oh," I said, stopping. "I forgot."

Jason handed me the take-away cup and a warm muffin in a container. I felt his warm blue eyes gazing at me, considering me. I felt as though I was the only person in the world. It left me shaken more than I already felt. I couldn't handle the scrutiny and wanted to slink away to a corner. I felt awful; a werewolf had bitten me and I was most probably dying. The last thing I needed was a man pestering me.

"Thanks," I whispered, turning away, avoiding his penetrating gaze.

"Take this," he said, his tone filled with concern, and slipped something into my pocket.

"What's that?" I asked, still staring at my feet.

"It's my business card with my cellphone number. Call me if you need anything. I mean it, Claire. Anything at all and any time. I want to help."

"I'm fine." I wasn't fine, but he didn't have to know.

Jason

Something was wrong. From the moment I walked to the front of the shop, I saw what I'd smelled only moments ago. An acrid stench that usually accompanied death assaulted my nose.

'*She's hurt,*' moaned my beast.

'*I know,*' I muttered my response.

'*We need to understand what happened,*' he whined.

I considered her; she hunched her shoulders over herself, her skin a gray color and the clothing she wore oversized and unflattering. Not that she couldn't wear it, but she was hiding herself away. And she was hurt—badly.

Ever since Claire had been coming into my coffee shop, we teased each other. It was fun, and I enjoyed speaking with her, even though I felt I irritated her, but I enjoyed pushing her buttons.

Whether she liked me, I didn't know. Perhaps she had an issue with were-animals. If that was the case, then I'd do everything in my power to change her mind. I wanted to get to know the little fiery vixen who sent my heart racing.

I'd even forgone dating other women because it just didn't sit right with me. The other women would flirt with me and try their luck, but I wasn't interested. The others from the pack said I was delusional and stupid for trying to persuade a human to like me, but I had to try.

I watched Claire slink away while I made her coffee and Mandy readied her muffin; I told her to add two, even though Claire had only ordered one.

When Mandy came out with the package, I took it from her and approached Claire carefully. I didn't want to frighten her, even though I did.

The moment Claire started dry-heaving, I knew something bad had happened. I smelled something on her I couldn't place; it was familiar, yet different. It had a bitter stench to it that reeked of something...

When Claire yelled she was fine and staggered away, I was glad I gave her my number. I doubted she'd use it though, but she had it, and I hoped she would call me.

It was a minute after three when I locked the shop

and greeted Mandy. I balanced the books and ordered more stock. By four o'clock I'd finished with my daily admin tasks, checked my phone for messages, but there were none and exited the back. Securing the back gate in place, I double checked the lock, then headed toward my vehicle.

I arrived at the Wolf Pack in time for our daily meeting. Shawn was our alpha leader and seemed more irritated than usual. He ran his fingers through his black hair, his blue eyes stared daggers at everyone, and the room vibrated with his power.

"What's up?" Killian asked, sitting down and putting his feet up on the next chair's armrest.

Shawn closed his eyes as he exhaled. His jaw ticked as he opened his eyes. I'd seen Shawn pissed off, but never this bad before, and wondered what had happened to set him off.

He leaned against the front of his desk, folded his arms, and finally spoke. "Troy contacted me. He says some of his lions sniffed a rogue were-wolf entering their territory. They tried to follow his stench but lost him late last night when he crossed into the leopard's territory. They didn't want to enter without permission, but they phoned Sebastian, who sent some leopards to find the rogue. Unfortunately, they lost him and now all the were's are on high alert." He cleared his throat, walked around his desk, and sat down. He rested his elbows on his desk, and steepled his fingers. "You all know how I despise this type of behavior. When we find this rogue wolf, we will destroy him—"

Sawyer burst through the doors with Mel behind him; their hair and clothing disheveled, as if they ran all the way here.

"What's going on?" Shawn commanded.

"We just saw Désiré, who alerted us to an incident at her hospital," Mel said, closing the distance and sitting beside me. She was a were-wolf and part of our pack. And she was one of the doctors who treated all the were's regardless of their flavor. She helped everyone in need.

Mel smiled at me in greeting before giving her attention back to our alpha. "A man visited the emergency room late last night." She paused for effect. "He was missing an eye and had scratch marks down his face. Désiré was on duty and tended to his wounds. She couldn't save his eye and when she asked him what happened, he was elusive and hurried to leave. Désiré says she knew he was a were-animal, just not which kind. She also added that a putrid smell clung to the walls in the room. She asked the cleaning crew to clean everywhere, but it still smells of him."

"He probably gave false details upon arrival. I don't suppose she can give us any information on him?" Shawn asked.

Sawyer, a British were-jackal we'd adopted, smiled. "She has something better," he said, handing Shawn a piece of paper.

"A picture," Shawn grinned. "It's grainy but we can still make out his features. We'll make print outs and send to everyone, including the WAA."

The WAA was the Were-Animal Alliance for Sterling Meadow; it comprised all the different shifters who lived in Sterling Meadow. We helped each other when in need. All our numbers were dwindling and by forging an alliance we hoped to keep each pack strong and safe. And we didn't want outsiders destroying our territories. We even had the vampires on our side, which deterred most from trying. But once in a while someone tried their luck... like now.

"We'll need everyone on this," Shawn continued. His mood better now that he had more information on this stranger who had everyone on high alert.

I wondered why the rogue was at the hospital.

"Did Désiré say why he was there? I mean, he was missing an eye. Does she know what happened," I asked.

"Apparently assaulted by a gang and got away," Sawyer said. "But he's lying." Everybody nodded in agreement.

My thoughts drifted to Claire and how she looked when she entered my shop. The coincidence of her appearance and this stranger seeking medical attention were too strong to ignore. I couldn't help but wonder if she met this newcomer. My anger seethed as I fisted my hands.

'We want Claire.' My beast whispered inside my head.

'I know. But if she's hurt, we must take care of her first.'

He harrumphed, not pleased with my answer.

Shawn continued with his plan. We were to separate into teams, and with the help of the other shifter animals, we hoped to find him tonight.

Claire

⚜

I entered the grocery store pushing a trolley to help keep myself upright. It was Saturday afternoon and quiet, which selfishly relieved me.

At the back of the store was a deli with some of the tastiest pastries, sandwiches, and cold meats. The woman behind the counter took my order and packed a box. While I waited, I grabbed some steaks and a bowl of fruit. The woman handed me my box, and I placed it in the trolley and wheeled over to the toiletries section. There they had a variety of over-the-counter treatments for wound care. Not knowing which was the best, I grabbed what I thought would help, along with butterfly bandages.

I passed the liquor aisle and added a bottle of

whiskey into my cart, a packet of crisps and a pint of ice-cream.

My hand shook as I paid for my groceries and was relieved everything fitted into two bags.

The walk back to my apartment felt surreal; the fever returning with a vengeance. As I traversed the sidewalk, it warped beneath my feet. I was sure I looked like someone walking on Mars. I felt as though I wore fish goggles and couldn't see my feet.

Sweat dripped down the sides of my face, and my heart raced inside my chest. A strange sound came from behind me. I didn't understand what it was, nor did I want to turn around for fear of falling over.

"Claire!" someone yelled, but I dared not stop.

The ground beneath me swirled. I leaned against the wall before I crashed to the ground.

"Claire? Are you okay?" someone asked but I couldn't see their face. My surroundings darkened as my fever split my head open and started spooning out my brain. I lurched forward and vomited on shoes standing in front of me.

"Oh, gods, I'm so sorry," I said, squinting at the person before me. I leaned my right knee against the wall and balanced the grocery bag while my right hand pulled off my sunglasses so I could see better. Once my glasses were off, I still couldn't see the person. The sun was shining directly into my eyeballs, blinding me. "Oh, no!" I blurted, as the world tipped to the side. I couldn't brace myself and landed on something cold, squishy, and wet.

Claire

The smell of steak frying brought me out of my dark dreams. I couldn't remember what I dreamed, but it left me drenched in perspiration once again.

"You have a fever, Claire," someone said, followed by quickened footsteps.

I opened my eyes and squinted at the person. I recalled his voice but couldn't place it. When he neared, I shot up in my seat.

"What are you doing here?" I grumbled. "You've made it perfectly clear you no longer want me. Now get out," I yelled the last part, pointing at my door. My head exploded in another bout of pain, as if speaking forced the volcanic eruptions in my veins to flood my brain.

"I'll go once you've eaten and taken some painkillers." Erik handed me a plate with a steak and a salad. He set the glass of water on the coffee table and sat in the one-seater across from me.

"Why do you even care?" I didn't bother with utensils and picked up the steak with my fingers, biting into it. It was slightly chewy but tasted divine.

"I wanted to apologize for the way I handled everything. I should've said something the last time we were together and not at the restaurant." He almost sounded sincere. *Almost.*

I exhaled a frustrated breath, hate simmering beneath the surface. "You cheated on me, Erik. If you'd just texted me you were breaking up, before you fucked her, it would've been better. I mean, you brought her with you last night. Why? So she could watch how you dump your girlfriend for her. What's wrong with you?" I yelled.

He was quiet for a while but didn't answer. It was a rhetorical question and didn't want him to answer, anyway.

We sat in silence while I ate, licking the juices off the plate. My hunger finally sated. My eyeballs burned, and I gathered it was the fever rearing its ugly head again. I grabbed the tablets and washed them down with water.

"There, I've eaten and taken my tablets. You can go now."

"What happened last night? I don't mean to sound cruel, but you look like shit."

"It's no longer your concern. Thanks for helping me into my apartment," — I grumbled, — "and feeding me. Now please go," I barked, giving him a deadpanned stare.

"I brought your stuff. And grabbed what was mine," he said and stood. "You can still call me if you need help with anything. I don't want us to be enemies—"

"You should've thought of that before you fucked someone else, Erik. Now get out!" I yelled, my voice croaking toward the end, but I refused to let him see me cry.

It would be easy to just give in and allow Erik to hold me and tell me it would all be okay. I could ask him to help me through whatever I was going through, and he would help. But I didn't want my heart ripped out again. To be rejected twice in a row —by the same man—would be too much for me to handle.

He stared with sympathy in his intense eyes, pursed his lips, and offered a curt nod. He closed the door softly behind him and I burst into tears.

———

A wolf with one glowing, gray eye chased me through the forest. I was ahead of the beast and just when I thought I found the path leading back to my apartment, it took me to another part of the forest I'd seen before. We ran around and around, but I couldn't escape the beast.

I felt exhausted. My body ached and my lungs burned. The wolf howled behind me, letting me know he was closing the distance.

Leaves crunched, and twigs snapped. I spun around and saw a naked man approach. His face obscured; a shiver down my back set off warning bells. The smell of pines and wet grass surrounded me, but as the man neared, I smelled musk and animal.

"What are you waiting for? Let go!" he said, his voice deep and commanding.

My arms pebbled the closer he came. I backed up against a tree with thick bushes surrounding me; there was no escaping him.

The man continued stalking me.

My breath caught in my throat, sweat dripped down my back, and an unknown rage filled my veins with ice.

"Let me in," he whispered in a low growl. "Let me ease your pain," he said huskily.

I jackknifed out of bed. My linen damp and knotted around me. I struggled with the sheet for a minute before finally untangling myself and jumped out of bed. The motion was so sudden, I flew and landed with a hard thud against the wall and fell to the floor. My shoulder ached and my forearm stung, letting me know I needed to clean the wounds again.

Once I caught my breath, I stood and fetched the new items I'd bought and removed the old dressing. In the mirror I saw the shoulder wound, red and inflamed. With my index finger and thumb, I pressed lightly on the raised welt. The wound opened further, with a white substance oozing out. The same happened with the wound on my forearm. My wounds were badly infected and I doubted the salve I had would help appropriately.

What I was doing wasn't working and needed help. I picked up my cellphone and with a shaky hand dialed Blaire's number and told her what had happened.

She cursed loudly and told me to hang on, putting me on hold.

While I waited, I sprayed the disinfectant on my forearm and it burned like Hell had released its evil tendrils into me, then I smeared some of the ointment on. The salve calmed the flames within my flesh, and I sat back against the bath.

"Claire? Claire, are you there?" Blaire yelled.

"Yeah," I croaked.

"I'm out of town on that case and can't get to you. Someone will fetch you," she said. "Don't worry, we'll get the evil wolf who did this and sort you out." She ended the call before I replied.

Tears welled in my eyes at her compassion, albeit a little scary, but she meant well. She cared for others, even though it was slightly on the aggressive side.

I packed an overnight bag and threw the bandages and ointment inside. When I set the bag near the door, someone knocked. I peeked through the peephole and groaned. Yanking open the door, finding Jason standing on the other side. Apart from his outward appeal, it was his grim expression that caught my attention. Anger radiated off him in waves, and I stepped back before I received a lashing.

"Blaire said you needed help," Jason said, but it came out like a growl.

"If you're angry about fetching me, you can just go. Tell me where I need to be and I'll get there myself."

His shoulders sagged and expression softened, but he still radiated fury. "I'm not angry about being here, Claire," he said my name so tenderly I almost cried. "I just wish you said something earlier at my shop when I asked. I could've helped you."

I exhaled and my shoulders slumped, but then pain shot through my neck and I winced. In that split second, Jason was there, ready to pick me up.

"I'm okay," I said, raising my hands to stop him from touching me.

"Where did he bite you?" Jason asked with concern in his ice-colored blue eyes.

I contemplated whether to tell him, but he'd find out, eventually. "My shoulder and forearm. I tried to clean the wounds but they're badly infected."

Sadness washed over him, and tears pricked my eyes. I didn't know why I was so emotional, but I fought to stop my chin from trembling.

"Do you understand what would happen after you're viciously bitten by a were-animal?" he asked carefully, like one would a frightened child.

I swallowed and blinked a few times. It hadn't dawned on me what would happen, if anything. I thought the wounds were just infected and needed cleaning; the worst that would happen to me was death. But now that he mentioned it, I almost collapsed.

Jason was there to pick me up before I crashed to the floor, and this time I didn't protest. He settled me on the closest chair and leaned before me, still holding my hand. My eyes flitted to his enormous hand and the corded muscles in his arm. Warmth radiated from him, and it felt like a comfort blanket surrounding me.

Before I'd always just dismissed his comments when I spoke to him in his shop. I didn't know he genuinely cared. But he had to have a reason for showing kindness. Everybody had an ulterior motive.

"I take that as a no," he said, his kind eyes drinking me in. "If you don't die from the attack, there's a chance you'll become the animal who bit you. I can help you with your change. Think of me as your were-buddy." His smile hinted at a tender side, and my chest tightened. Not liking the sensation, guilt rocked through me. Or was it denial? Regardless, I didn't like how his kind words made me feel.

"Why?"

"Why what?"

"Why would you help me? I've always been so bitchy to you."

He laughed. "I don't see it that way. I always look forward to your daily visits and bantering. Besides, I don't give up easily when I know what I want." His tone was serious but his blue eyes held humor and something else I couldn't decipher.

My breath caught in my throat, and I struggled to swallow. No-one had ever said that to me before, not even Erik. I didn't understand what he meant and didn't think it was the right time to ask for details. My body ached as a volcano erupted inside my head.

"Thank you," I said, wincing.

"Come, the sooner Mel treats you, the better."

"Where are we going?"

"To the Wolf Pack."

Jason

Once Claire climbed into my car and settled into her seat, she fell asleep. Her body seemed so small and fragile in the oversized clothing, it left me worried.

Although I knew little about her, I wanted to change that, and I'd do everything I could to bring her justice. I wanted to find the rogue were-wolf and kill him for what he did to her. No human should have their choice made for them and attacking someone to change them was against everything I believed in.

Claire stirred as she fought demons in her dream, or nightmare. Sweat peppered her forehead and when I stopped at a red light, I wiped her brow. Her face hot to the touch, yet she shivered.

The moment the light changed to green I smashed

the gas; I had to get to the Wolf Pack. Mel needed to tend to her wounds immediately.

It angered me that she didn't ask for help, but I got the sense she was as stubborn as they came. When I asked her whether she understood what it meant to be bitten. I didn't think she fully comprehended that she would turn into a wolf on a monthly basis, and for the rest of her life. But only if she survived the fever. From the looks of it, she was struggling. I hoped Mel could save her in time.

Five minutes later, I stopped outside the Wolf Pack, opened her car door, and scooped her in my arms. Still asleep, she burned against my chest and arms. But I didn't want to let her go, nor did I want anyone else carrying her.

Once inside the building, Mel called me to the area where she tended to the injured wolves. I entered the room and placed Claire gently on the table.

"Thanks, I'll let you know when I'm done."

"I'm not leaving her," I grumbled. "I'm staying to help."

She narrowed her piercing brown eyes at me that would usually make wolf pups run with their tails between their legs, but I didn't care. I wasn't going anywhere.

"What is she to you? Blaire called me to help her.

You just drove her over. It was something a lesser wolf should've done, not a senior alpha."

"I see her every day at my shop. We speak all the time." I cleared my throat. "I'm helping you, and I'll be here when she wakes up. You know, so she sees a friendly face. She doesn't know anyone else."

Mel grunted with a thin smile creeping up her face, but said nothing else.

When Blaire phoned Shawn, I was with him in his office, going over the map where others had spotted the rogue were-wolf. We'd placed red pins into the various locations and then we contacted others to check out the spots where we thought the rogue might have gone to rest. Since Désiré couldn't help him with his eye, he was now blind on one side and would need to rest somewhere to heal—either by shifting into his beast or slower as a human.

Désiré said whoever had clawed out his eye had damaged his eye socket, the cranial nerves, blood vessels and ligaments. She even pulled out two broken nails that were embedded inside his flesh. I shuddered when I heard that—it must've hurt. I couldn't imagine what Claire had experienced as she clawed at the rogue. He deserved worse.

My heart sank to my toes when I really thought about what that rogue had done to her.

'Release me so I can sniff out this rogue. I want to kill him.' My beast thought.

'Me too, Beast! Let's first hear what really happened.'

I cleared my throat and asked Mel as delicately as possible.

"Uh, Mel?"

"Hmm."

"I'll leave the room when you do this… but… we might need to see whether he sexually assaulted her."

Mel widened her eyes and glanced down at Claire. "Oh, I didn't know."

"I don't either, but we need to make sure she's okay… everywhere." I motioned over Claire's unconscious body.

Mel nodded. "Yes, yes, of course," she stammered as she cut through Claire's clothing. "I'd prefer if you weren't here when I remove her clothing. We might be comfortable with each other's nakedness, but I don't know if she is. The last thing I want is to violate her further."

"Of course, but please call me when she's covered, and I can come back inside to help you where you need me."

I left Mel to do her thing, but stood outside the door with my arms crossed over my chest.

Shawn exited his office and approached. "How is she?"

"Don't know, but I think it's bad."

"Are you staying here all day?"

"I'm waiting for Mel, then I'll go back inside and help her."

Shawn furrowed his brows. "Why do you care about this human? She works for Blaire, not you."

"Why does everyone ask me that? She comes into my shop. I know her."

"So that's why you jumped at fetching her; usually it's a job for one of the younger wolves. I was curious as to the reason." Shawn grinned, then he sobered. "We'll get this guy—"

"I want him," I demanded, while Beast growled inside my head. My pulse thundered in my ears and my heart stuttered.

Shawn's eyebrows shot up. Then he narrowed his eyes. "How much do you like her?"

"Well, we'll see if she likes me as much as I like her. Regardless of her decision, though, I still want this guy. I want him to pay for what he did to her." My thoughts crashed to the possibility of the rogue doing more than just biting her, but that wouldn't stop me from claiming her. The thought caught me off guard. I'd never wanted to claim her, but now that the winds have whispered it, I'd made my decision. I wanted her, and I would claim her. And I'd do everything necessary so she saw me—the man—and not just the beast. But one of my kind had hurt her, and she might want nothing to do with me afterwards. It would challenge me, but I never shied away from any problem. I'd take anything she dished with a smile on my face.

"Okay." He placed a calm hand on my shoulder. "He's all yours. And be ready. Our guys are scouting in all the nooks and crannies for this douche bag, and I'm sure we'll get him soon." Shawn dropped his arm to his side, gave a curt nod, and then headed back to his office.

The door clicked behind me, and Mel peered through the small opening. "You can come in now."

I followed behind Mel while she spoke. "I didn't find any trauma," she said. "And I didn't think it worth her discomfort for an internal exam. If anything had happened, I would've seen."

I nodded my understanding. "Thanks, Mel," I said with relief. Even if he had sexually assaulted her, it wouldn't stop me from pursuing her, and I'd be there for her every step of the way during her recovery. If she allowed, I'd be available to her in any way she wanted.

My breath caught in my throat when I saw the wound on her shoulder and forearm. I didn't know how serious it was because of the oversized clothing she'd worn. I stood closer for a better look. Her collar bone was visible, with torn muscles and a white substance covering them.

"Is this supposed to happen?" I asked, pointing at the white stuff.

"I think our rogue is suffering from some infection. Or, her body is fighting the change. We won't know until I get it tested."

"Will she wake up when we clean?"

"No, I've given her something to help with the pain and to keep her from waking," Mel said, moving around the table. "Let's start. Once we've cleaned the areas, we'll know how serious her condition is. The sooner we get her bandaged, the sooner she's on the road to recovery," Mel said with a concerned smile that didn't reach her eyes.

During the next hour, I did everything Mel asked me to do. I cleaned where she pointed and fetched the items she needed while she cut dead flesh away and sutured Claire's shoulder; her focus on the patient.

I handled Claire with tenderness, even though she was asleep. She'd gone through enough pain and trauma. I didn't want to add to it.

With Claire's shoulder wound sutured closed, Mel added the potent ointment she used on were-animals to help us heal quicker. Within minutes Claire's skin changed; it was no longer an angry red or as inflamed.

Next was her forearm. I cringed at the exposed muscle and the ripped pieces of flesh dangling from one side. Mel cut the pieces away, cleaned, and stitched everything together.

I watched Claire stir in her sleep but didn't wake. She rested peacefully, but her closed eyes moved as if searching for something. Low mewling sounds escaped her lips, while her breathing became irregular. It relieved me she didn't stop breathing altogether.

I held her hand to feel her pulse, and I hoped she felt warmth from my grip. Mel kept glancing at our hands, but I didn't pull away. I didn't care who saw.

"You like this girl?" Mel asked with a smirk. "She is pretty."

"It's not just that. She's sweet for someone with a large bark," I said as I considered the sleeping, injured girl. Her hand rested limply in my larger one.

For the last six months, Claire had been coming into my coffee shop. The first few times she was a little shy, then when I started speaking to her, she became grumpy. Then our bantering continued daily. It was a conversation I looked forward to. She was the sun my body yearned for, the water to quench my thirst, and the nourishment for my health.

When I heard she'd started working for Blaire, it elated me. That meant I'd be seeing more of her. I'd hoped Blaire would take her with on assignments and join us at the WAA meetings. But she never did. That didn't stop me from looking forward to our brief morning chats.

Claire

My skin tingled, muscles ached, and my body heavy. I shifted on the soft surface without needing to recoil from the sensation.

My eyes flitted open, revealing a strange room I'd never seen before and couldn't remember how I got here or what I was doing before I slept.

I exhaled and shifted on the bed. My shoulder felt tight, and my arm stung as I flexed my fingers. When a powerful hand gripped mine, I froze. A face came into view; one I recognized. I yanked my hand out of his and tried to sit up. The sudden movement shot pain laced with venom through my body, and I winced, lying back down. The memories came flooding back like a Tsunami on steroids and I recalled the attack, the pain, and Jason fetching me.

"Rest. You're safe. I got you," he said gently. His hand still enveloping mine.

I stared daggers at Jason. "Why are you gawking at me? Shouldn't you be out chasing critters?" I was a terrible person for saying that to him after everything he did for me. But it was his kind that attacked me, even though I knew it wasn't his fault. I was in pain and miserable. And he was giving me a look I couldn't understand. It left me uncomfortable.

His deep laugh vibrated through the bed and into my chest. "I might go later, but right now I'm not hungry for food. Thanks for asking." He winked.

I clucked my tongue. "What did the doctor say? Am I going to live?" I obviously knew I'd live, other-wise, I'd be dead. I said that so he would quit staring at me. But it didn't work.

"There's no easy way to say this," he started, then sighed, but his eyes twinkled. "The bad news is the bites were deep, obviously. He took sizable chunks out of you. And you'll live. The good news is you'll turn into a wolf at the next full moon. All is not lost. If you like, I'm offering you a once in a lifetime deal. I'll guide you every step of the way... if you want?" His expression softened as ice filled my veins.

I bolted upright, and stars exploded before my eyes. I winced from the pain but shoved it down. What Jason just told me was worse than the aches I currently had. "Good news? Are you crazy? I'm going to become a mutt. No, no, no..." I mumbled over and over, followed by curse words.

I tried to swing my legs off the bed to get up, but powerful hands kept me down.

"No sudden movements," Jason grunted, making all the hairs on my arms stand up. "Give yourself a couple of minutes to adjust before you jump up and run away."

"I wasn't trying to run away," I grumbled.

He arched an eyebrow.

I scowled at him. He didn't react. I exhaled a frustrated breath.

The more I thought about it, the more I knew he was right, which only made me hate him more. I stopped resisting.

"I'll take you home the moment you don't see stars," he continued calmly. "If you want, ask me questions. I know you might have a couple, and I'll tell you everything."

Tears welled in my eyes, and I didn't care that he saw them. "I can't believe this is happening to me," I whimpered.

"And for your information, we are not mutts," he said amusingly, ignoring my outburst. "We are majestic animals—"

"Pfft, whatever, that's your opinion, not mine," I grumbled.

His smile lit up his face and as contagious as it

was, I dared not give in, but couldn't help it, and smiled.

"There we go," he said, brushing his thumb against my cheek. I felt the calluses against my skin, which helped me relax. I leaned into his hand and closed my eyes. He was so warm and gentle. When I realized what I was doing, I bolted upright and scowled at him, which made him laugh harder. "We aren't the enemy, Claire. And I certainly am not. I will be here for you through everything, if you'll let me."

"Don't you have a wife or a girlfriend to pester?" My brows furrowed as I stared into his blue eyes; they were the lightest blue I'd ever seen and shivered.

"No." He shook his head. "Not for a long time."

"Why?"

Jason opened his mouth to answer when a large, bulky man strode in like he owned the place. His hair was so dark it brought out the color of his eyes, reminding me of glaciers, coupled with the stern expression that left me feeling intimidated. I sat back on the bed and pulled the covers up to my chest.

"This is Shawn, our alpha," Jason said.

"How are you feeling? Blaire keeps bugging me, so the sooner I tell her the sooner I can get her off my ass," Shawn said. His expression softened, but I remained guarded.

"I don't know. I think I'm okay." I shrugged, thinking about how I really felt—which was much better than I did yesterday, or whenever it felt like I was dying. "How long have I been here?"

"About two hours," Jason added.

"Good, at least you're feeling okay instead of worse." Shawn smiled. "I take it Jason has given you the news and allow me to be the first to welcome you to the Wolf Pack, if you wish to join us. And to let you know we're still hunting down the rogue wolf who attacked you."

"You know who he is?"

Shawn nodded. "We have a grainy picture of him and circulated copies to all the were-animals. We'll find him. And he's missing an eye, so he'll be hard to miss," he grinned.

My throat ached as I swallowed, realizing these people were doing this for me. But I guessed they'd do it regardless of whether he had attacked me. This wolf was a rogue and could hurt one of their own. I shouldn't feel that special. But I couldn't come across as rude and unappreciative of their hospitality.

"I'm glad he lost an eye." I recalled the memory of digging my fingers into his eye socket.

"It was quite the destruction. One of our doctors who treated him at the ER said you even managed to damage some nerves inside the socket," Shawn added.

"Good, and thank you for everything. I don't know what I would've done..." my voice trailed as thoughts of dying crashed into me; the pain alone could've been the end of me. What they did for me was priceless. They didn't know me, yet they did everything in their power to save me. I should be kinder to Jason, but—

"It's our pleasure," Shawn said, bringing me out of my thoughts. "It was the least we could do. We don't tolerate attacks or changing humans against their will. It was wrong and punishable by death. We will torture this guy before we end him." His words made my arms pebble, and I couldn't wait. "I must go. Jason has volunteered to buddy with you through the change. Allow him to help you, Claire. I know you're strong willed, but you will need him. It's not something you'd want to go alone."

Unsure of my words, I just nodded and averted my eyes to stare at my bandaged forearm. I glanced up my arm and noted I wore a dressing gown that was an improvement on those available in hospitals. My brows shot up when I realized I was naked underneath.

"Did you undress me?" I asked Jason and was glad Shawn had already left.

One side of his mouth curled upward when he answered. "Maybe."

My cheeks heated and was sure I glowed red.

Jason must've noted my discomfort and patted my thigh. "I left the room while Mel undressed you. I saw nothing. I swear."

I pulled the covers tighter against my body. "Good," I said, my frown still on my face. "Can you take me home now?" I asked, wanting to go home and rest.

"Is there anyone I should call to let them know you're okay? Like that guy I saw you with in my shop last week?"

The lines between my brows deepened. Last week Jason was busy in the back, and I didn't think he saw me with Erik. We'd stopped by to grab coffee before our movie. It was no use lying to Jason, he'd find out I no longer had anyone in my life.

"He broke up with me last night before our anniversary dinner," I said. "He cheated on me and brought the girl with him as backup," I snorted, which was very unladylike. "To answer your question, *no*. I'm no longer dating anyone. And there's nobody to call." I exhaled sadly.

He smiled as if it was good news.

My heart fluttered inside my chest at the possibilities but pushed them down. *No.*

"Good, then you'll stay here for a bit. Mel said you should rest. She's still here in case you need her. Relax for a few more hours, then I'll take you home."

I sighed, but knew he wasn't going to budge on

the subject. And perhaps he was right. I'd give it a few hours and then bug him until he took me home.

Jason

There was no way I'd drop Claire off near her apartment building and just drive away like she'd asked me to. I had to ensure she was safely inside her home, and everything was secure.

She had healed quickly, and we left earlier than I wanted to. Mel had said it was because of the wolf gene taking hold of her system and turning her into a wolf. The change would be gradual and scary, and she'd need me to guide her. She still hadn't answered me about whether she wanted to buddy with me, but I understood she had to ask out of her own. I couldn't force her. But this, ensuring she was safe, I wouldn't budge on.

When she opened her apartment door, she almost

closed it in my face, but my foot had stopped it from shutting. I growled. She rolled her eyes. My palm itched to smack her ass, but thought it best not to... not yet. I grinned at the thought.

Beast whined in the metaphysical realm where he roamed, waiting to be set free when I called upon him.

I stepped over the threshold and closed the door behind me. Her living area and kitchen were one large space, with one bathroom and one bedroom. There was clothing on the floor, her bed unmade and the kitchen dirty. It reminded me of when I had a bachelor pad. At least she wasn't the type to clean every crumb. That would drive me mad. Sometimes there was order in chaos.

"There's no point in trying to hide the dirty stuff." She dropped the shirt she picked up. "I just don't have the energy to clean now," she said when she noted me staring at her clothing on the floor.

"I can help."

"No, I don't want you touching my dirty under-wear or snooping in my closet. But thanks anyway. You can go now."

"Claire!"

"What, Jason? The big evil wolf doesn't know where I live..." the rest of her words caught in her throat as her expression went blank. She glanced nervously at me, then at the bag filled with the bandages she'd brought with her. I placed it on the coffee table. She approached the bag and opened it, shaking her head.

"What's wrong? What are you looking for?"

"I need to go to the park," she said, eyes wide. I heard her racing heart. She shut her eyes and bit her lip. There was something missing. The first thing I thought of was her purse. She'd dropped it some-where, and if she left it where the rogue had attacked her, she was in trouble.

Beast pushed to the surface.

'Not yet, buddy. Soon.' I thought, trying to calm him.

"Did you drop your bag or purse with your details inside?"

"I must've," she said, chewing on her bottom lip. "We used my other set of keys I keep in my bag with some cash," — she pointed at the bag on the coffee table, — "But, I don't remember coming home Friday night or how I got inside but I keep a spare key on top of the door frame."

Without her asking, I inspected the door frame and shook my head. Her spare key gone.

Her eyes darted across the open living area, and kitchen until she settled on something. The spare key; on the floor beside a coffee table leg.

"I think we should see if your bag is still there."

I feared for her life if she stayed here. If that rogue had her personal information, there was no doubt in my mind he'd come looking for her to finish the job —especially since she'd taken his eye—he'd want revenge. I'd want revenge if that had happened to me.

"You can't stay here anymore—"

"Before we panic, can we first see if it's at the park?"

We exited her apartment building in silence. She worked her bottom lip with her top teeth and when we reached my car; I smelled blood. She'd punctured her lip and pressed her finger to the cut.

"I know this is your home, but there's a place for you at the Wolf Pack. Stay there for a few days or until we find this guy. It will be good for you to be near us. If you don't want my help, there are others you can go to," I said as I climbed inside my vehicle and started the engine. I tried not to sound agitated, but I was. She needed to understand the gravity of her situation.

Claire stared nervously at me, but said nothing. Sweat peppered her forehead, which she wiped away with the back of her hand.

I drove the short distance to the park, found a parking spot near the entrance, and we headed toward the area where she thought he had attacked her. It was just after six in the evening and kids were still playing ball or throwing a frisbee while families lounged on the grass.

The sun glowed a bright orange as it settled on the horizon, painting the sky bright colors of pinks, yellows, and reds.

Claire stood near a disturbed area; they had kicked tufts of grass out with sandy patches. We searched near trees and brushes where she could've dropped her bag, but there was nothing. A man wearing a green uniform and holding a rake approached us. I flagged him down and asked if he'd seen a bag lying around or if anyone had handed one over. He shook his head and mumbled 'no', arching an eyebrow in Claire's direction. I stood in front of her, blocking his view. He grumbled as he passed us.

"That was odd."

"Tell me about it. Come," — I grabbed hold of Claire's good elbow, — "let's get out of here. If you left your bag here, it's gone now. You might have to call your bank to cancel your card and order a new one."

"I didn't have any bank cards, just cash and business cards. But I may have written my address on the back of my business cards for deliveries," she said, hugging herself.

I placed my hand on the small of her back, leading her away from the park. She didn't push me away or complain, so I left my hand there, feeling her back muscles move as she walked.

For now, there was nothing we could do about her missing purse. All I knew I couldn't leave her alone. I'd have to watch over her or get her to stay at the Wolf Pack for a few days.

Once back at her apartment, I hesitantly opened the door to leave. I gathered she needed some space and would give it to her.

"Do you have enough food? I can drop something off when I pop in again later."

"I'll be fine, thanks," she said. Her voice quiet with a hint of sadness that clung to my heart. I cursed these emotions and welcomed them at the same time. It felt as though I was tearing apart; I wanted to be there for her, but also wanting to give her her space. She needed to approach me if she wanted my help.

"You have my number," I added. I made sure she punched in my number and the main phone number for the Wolf Pack. She'd said it amazed her she still had her phone, and had most likely tucked it into her jeans that evening.

"Yes, thanks. I'll let you know if I need anything. I just want to lie down."

"I'll see you soon to change the lock. But call for anything. And if you have questions—"

"I know, I know. I'll call you." She touched my shoulder, gently nudging me out the door.

As I walked to my vehicle, the feeling of her hand on my shoulder continued to burn my skin as if she were still beside me.

Claire

Jason was adamant that he walked me directly to my apartment both times he brought me home. I appreciated his help, but all I wanted to do was rest. My wounds ached even though I felt better. My insides twisted as if something was taking a hold of me. And my skin crawled like tiny insects were biting me.

When Jason finally left, I locked the door and stared at my hand. There was a strange tingling sensation from when I gently pushed him out of my apartment. Making a fist, then opening my hand again to stop the prickling, but it lingered. I shrugged it off to the changes relating to my body and headed toward my bedroom.

My bedding was slightly damp and in need of another change. I removed the previous set from the washing machine and threw them into the dryer, added the soiled set to the washing machine and switched it on. Now I had nothing else to put on the mattress.

I pulled a blanket out of the closet and threw it over the mattress, climbed onto the bed, and tucked my pillow into my neck. The moment I closed my eyes, I fell into a deep sleep.

———

Dark clouds moved swiftly across the sky, covering the pale moon. Howling echoed through the night, causing the hairs all over my body to stand on end.

Jason stood beside me, partially shifted into his much larger beast, leaving me awestruck by his dangerous beauty.

"Are you ready, Claire?" he asked with a deep baritone through a large, toothy jaw. His face now furry while his usual blue eyes glowed bright yellow/green. He pointed his dark claws toward a hair-raising path in the forest.

"I'm scared," I croaked, trying in vain to swallow my fear.

"I've got you." His voice reverberated in my chest, and I knew he meant it. He would not leave me, nor hurt me. I knew in my heart he'd protect me with his powerfully built body and cared for me in ways no one had ever before, even though we hardly knew each other.

I turned to give him my attention when he ripped his already torn jeans from his body to afford him the space to shift into his white wolf. His change was effortless, and I doubted he no longer felt pain. One second he was still in his half-beast, the next he stood beside; his head reaching my hips.

I smiled down at him but doubted he saw me as he stalked toward the area we were about to travel. Jason was the size of a small pony and his muscles moved powerfully beneath his fur. I couldn't help myself as I watched in amazement.

The clouds moved away from the moon, blasting me with its silver tendrils. Jason said the full moon wouldn't command my first change but it would help it along, and it did so with vengeance. My skin seared off my body as if someone took a blowtorch to me. My tendons and bones snapped, sending bolts of electricity throughout my veins, and I fell to the ground on all fours. I roared instead of screamed as my body broke, then readjusted itself.

When I opened my eyes, one white eye stared back at me. My hackles raised, fearing danger as the creature before me pounced. He crashed into me, and I jackknifed out of bed, fighting with the blanket.

My clothing stuck to my skin, my breathing

labored, and all I wanted to do was get out of the knot I'd made for myself.

Someone pounded on the door, followed by yelling.

I finally untangled myself out of my bedding, stumbled out of bed, and crashed to the floor. "I'm coming," I yelled, trying to stand. "Just stop banging on the door." My legs felt like jello, so instead of standing I crawled toward the front door.

The pounding continued, with Jason yelling on the other side. "Claire? Claire?"

"Christ, I'm coming," I moaned, using the wall to help me stand and unlocked the door. "You don't have to break the door down."

"If I wanted to break the door, I wouldn't have knocked lightly," he grumbled. His chest rising and falling, and his eyes glowed. "Where were you?" he asked. A flurry of emotions crossed his face as he entered my apartment.

"I was sleeping. Jeez, give a girl a break." I rubbed my thighs as the feeling in my legs returned.

"How are you feeling?" He threw a bag onto the floor and removed tools and a box.

"Better, what's that?" I asked, frowning.

"I'm changing your locks and installing an alarm." He pulled the items out of the box. Then ushered me out of the way so he could get to the door.

"Thanks," I said. "You're really going out of your way to help me, Jason. I don't know what to say."

"Let me help you through the change," he said without looking at me. He unscrewed the current lock on the door, removed it, and set it one side.

"If that rogue finds me, I doubt these simple locks are going to keep him out. You said it yourself you could break it down."

"It would still give you time to get away. Or get help."

I couldn't think of an answer fast enough, so I thought it best to keep quiet. He was right.

We fell into a comfortable silence as I watched him work on the door. I sat on the couch, getting comfortable. My eyes not leaving his body. His corded arm muscles bunched as he twisted the screwdriver to install the new lock, testing that it was in place before starting on the other side.

I watched the muscles beneath his shirt move with strength I couldn't even imagine. His hair was short on the sides, neatly trimmed around his ears, and cut short on top. His beard was neatly trimmed, but I could see the sharp jaw beneath as the muscles ticked there. I wondered whether he felt my stare. And somewhere along the line, I salivated as I watched him and shifted uncomfortably.

Once the new lock was in, the alarm installed and activated, only then did Jason turn toward me. He raised both eyebrows. I felt exposed beneath his penetrating gaze, and I squirmed.

"Your fangs are out."

"What?" I asked, feeling the inside of my mouth with my tongue. My eyes widened as my tongue felt the sharp points of my canines. "Already?" I said with a lisp. They felt foreign inside my mouth, yet confusingly comfortable. I curled my lips to feel the sharp edges with my fingers and instead of crying, I smiled. "It's weird." I closed my mouth and wiped my fingers on my clothing. "Are you, uh… were you bitten?"

He smiled warmly and sat in the chair closest to me. "I'm a purebred. My parents were were-wolves and had a few pups. When I turned eighteen, I moved to Sterling Meadow, and loyal to Shawn ever since he became the alpha."

"And you're somewhere high in the pack order I gather?"

He nodded. "I'm third, but I'm happy to serve. I'm an alpha in my own right but I don't have to be *the* Alpha."

"And you age slowly?"

"Yes."

"How old are you?"

He grinned. "I'm double your age."

I furrowed my brows. "You don't know my age."

"You're thirty-seven, aren't you?"

I did one of those slow blinks as I mulled over his words. "Yeees, so that makes you what? Seventy-four?"

His grin remained plastered on his face. He sat against the chairback as if waiting for me to be repulsed by the fact he was in his seventies, but oh-my-gods he didn't look it.

"You look like you're thirty-something."

"That's right. Those bitten and changed age slowly, but purebreds age at a much slower rate. But I'm not immortal, I will die one day. Unless someone fights me and wins."

"But I doubt that will happen. You look like you can beat the crap out of everyone." My eyes flitted toward his chest and I waited for him to flex his pec muscles or something to show off but he didn't. Instead his smile morphed into a smirk, as if he knew what I was thinking. I schooled my features and waited for his answer.

"I'm a skilled fighter, and if you like, I can teach you. And if your fangs have already elongated, that means your change will happen a lot sooner than I thought."

"How come?"

"Everybody changes at their own pace. And I guess your body has taken to the wolf gene much easier. Have you thrown up much? Is your stomach in knots? Or do you have any other symptoms?"

"I'm nauseated but I haven't thrown up since that first night," I said as I thought about it. I was okay; my body ached, I felt drained, and my stomach was in knots. But I wasn't as bad as I was before. And I felt stronger.

"That's good," he said, standing up. "I'd like to stay here for the night. If that's okay with you?"

"What? Why?"

"Everybody is looking for this rogue wolf," he said gravely. "If he does come here, at least I'm close enough to help you."

I wasn't sure I wanted him in my personal space while my body changed. I didn't know what to expect or what would happen to my body. If I ripped my clothing off, I didn't want him gawking at me. But... if that rogue found his way here, I doubted I could fight him by myself, even with my newfound strength. I still didn't like the idea of Jason in my apartment and using my bathroom or opening my fridge.

When I was quiet for too long, he spoke. "It's just for the night—"

"No." I shook my head. "I know you mean well, but not tonight. I feel like I want to crawl out of my skin, and I don't want an audience."

"But I can help ease the pain."

"Thanks, but no. Please," I pleaded.

He exhaled and his shoulders dropped before he

inhaled. His mouth pulled in a tight line, and I knew I pissed him off.

"Can I ask you something?"

"Sure."

"Did you always know I was a were-wolf?" he asked, changing the subject.

It was a strange question, but I did. "Yes, why do you ask?"

"What happened? Who hurt you?" he asked with concern in his tone.

The question caught me off guard and I didn't want to answer it. "I think you should leave," I said, standing up and opening the door.

He raised both hands in surrender. "Sorry, I didn't mean to put you on the spot. I know our bantering was fun whenever you came into the coffee shop, but I couldn't help noticing the underlining hostility. Is it just towards were-wolves or all were-animals?" he asked with kindness.

It was true. When I realized he was a were-wolf, my demeanor shifted toward bitterness. It wasn't at him personally, but what had happened before.

"I'm sorry."

My frown was back, along with my left hand on my hip. "Why are you sorry? You did nothing."

"Whoever hurt you, tainted you for the rest of us. When you get to know me, you'll see I'm not so bad," he said solemnly and picked up his bag. "And

I'm not going away, Claire," he said my name with heartfelt emotion. His words seemed to wrap itself around my body, leaving goosebumps in its wake.

"Thank you." Was all I could say. I couldn't tell him what had happened to me, yet, and I hadn't said a word to anyone since it happened, nor did I want to. And what he'd said was true. It had ruined me for every shifter. Ever since it happened, I wanted nothing to do with shifters; they were much stronger than humans and could hurt us with a snap of their fingers.

I thought I would be all right. I thought I would see past my experience and look for the man beneath the animal, but I couldn't. I didn't want to get hurt again. That's probably the reason I chose Erik, who had a soft nature about him, and very human. Yet he hurt me in another way.

"I'll see you in the morning." Jason stood by the door, testing the locks one last time, and ensured the alarm worked. Before he closed the door, he added. "If you need me, I'm in my truck. And don't worry, I sleep little anyway. If you need anything, you know my vehicle. I'll be right outside."

"Thanks, but it's unnecessary."

He didn't answer, instead he closed the door softly behind him and I locked it.

Claire

The forest trees blurred past as I ran. My furry body moving faster than I ever did on two legs. My stomach full from the feast and everything felt right. Everything was going to go perfectly.

The chill of the night kept me comfortable as I pushed my body to move faster. Then something called to me. I stopped and headed in the sound's direction, following the calls to a waterfall.

They called my name again, but from behind the waterfall and within the rock. I didn't want to go into the dark, but something lured me inside.

Carefully, I jumped up onto the rocks, my sharp claws gripping the rough surface as I maneuvered along the ledge toward the waterfall. The water cascaded down, creating calming sounds. The calls echoed again, and I headed toward the darkness but didn't enter. As I reached the entrance, a large, dark claw reached for me.

I awoke with a start and on the floor. Somehow, I'd fought with my blanket again and was on the ground beside my bed. Staring up at the off-white ceiling, I made a mental note to have my landlady paint the apartment. I suspected the person before me had smoked a lot, leaving the walls a sickly yellow.

Pushing myself off the ground, I stood on shaky legs. Pain laced my abdomen, forcing me to double over. I gripped my stomach as I dry-heaved. My skin prickled, and the overall sensation left a sour taste in my mouth. I shuddered and pushed forward to at least reach the bathroom.

I had no concept of time, but suspected it was early morning. The street outside was quiet for an early Sunday, but especially for my apartment building. Usually there was someone blasting music till the sun rose, but not today.

I needed a shower; I stripped naked and considered my reflection in the mirror. The old deep scars scattered across my body had lightened somewhat, but were still visible. My skin no longer pale while my face wasn't as gaunt as it was yesterday. I felt better, albeit a little shaky. I suspected the were-wolf gene had already melded with my DNA, and I was slowly becoming one of them.

I hadn't thought about it; that I would become a were-wolf. It was much easier living in denial. But my body was changing. I could no longer live in ignorant bliss, no matter how tempting it was.

Eventually I'd have to accept the fact that I was changing and needed to somehow embrace it. The irony of my situation was not lost on me; the man I had loved had been a were-wolf. I wanted to be with him forever, but he had changed, and he had hurt me. Literally scarring me for life.

The scorching water massaged my aching muscles as I washed my hair twice; the sensation felt wonderful. Every time I massaged my scalp, waves of goosebumps spread across my skin as if someone was blowing their breath gently against me.

Once content my hair was clean, I washed my body. Then visions of Jason standing naked behind me flashed through my mind. His hands running up and down my sides, his fingers lightly caressing my breasts, then his hands moved down and squeezed my waist. Then more impressions of him breathing against my neck as his hands roamed over my body. The feel of his touch felt like velvet caresses as he kissed my neck.

My eyes shot open, and I stepped aside to make

sure he wasn't there. It all felt real, but it was only in my mind.

Confused by my arousal for the man/beast I hardly knew, yet curious as to his true intensions. Was he genuine in what he'd said, that he wasn't going anywhere and he'd never hurt me? I wanted to believe him. I wanted to trust him. As much as I subconsciously wanted him. My need to protect my body and my heart was more important.

I felt starved for attention even though I'd dated Erik for six months. What he and I had was different; less physical attraction, more communication. Little did that help though, he still cheated on me.

As much as I craved affection, I was afraid. But at the same time I wanted to let go of my inhibitions and say, *"Fuck it, let me see where this takes me."* Yet, I remained overly cautious.

If I thought carefully about it, I was attracted to Jason. It was the thought of him being a were-animal that stopped anything from happening. But, I was slowly changing my mind. I was changing.

I exhaled a frustrated breath and finished washing.

Once dressed, I opened my front door and checked both sides of the hallway. It was clear. I ran down the stairs three steps at a time without my shins paining and exited the building.

I wanted to ask Jason to come upstairs, for what I

didn't know. Perhaps I wanted to test myself and whether I really liked him and to gauge his reaction if I were to advance on him. I hadn't decided whether I'd do it.

As he promised, Jason had parked his black truck near the front of the doors to my apartment building and he stared straight at me. He stiffened when he recognized me and climbed out of his truck, meeting me before I took another step.

"That was fast," I said with a sly grin.

"What are you doing out here?" he asked, gripping my upper arms and stepped me backward.

I lifted my arms to bat him away from me, and he let go. "I couldn't sleep. And I wanted to see if you were really outside." I lied. But couldn't come up with anything else at that moment.

"I said I would," he said, sounding hurt by my insinuation.

"Do you want to come upstairs… for coffee?" I thumbed the building behind me.

He was quiet for a moment, then finally said. "I'd much rather open the shop." He glanced at his watch. It was almost five in the morning.

As much as I wanted him to come upstairs with me. Perhaps it wasn't the right time. He may have thought so too.

My smile split my face in two. "Good idea, I love your coffee." I exhaled a nervous breath as relief washed over me. If I was to let this man/beast into my life, I should take it slow instead of rushing to get naked; no matter how desperately I craved his touch. And I liked him more for taking the initiative. My chest warmed at the thought.

"Well, I'm glad there's something we can agree on," he said, winking wickedly.

His grin left my heart fluttering in my rib cage, and his blue eyes twinkled. He offered me his elbow, which I hesitated to take at first, but then slipped my hand through. I stepped closer to his warm body, resting my head against his arm. His free hand covering mine on his arm.

If anyone had to walk past us, they'd assume we were like any other young couple in love.

Jason's actions felt strange and although in the past I would've recoiled, I was slowly warming up to him. But my guard would remain up. He was larger than me, and definitely stronger. And he could still hurt me.

I swallowed the nervous lump and squeezed his fingers entwined with mine.

He shot me a sideways glance, and his lips curved at the side I could see. "I won't hurt you, Claire. I promise," he said, as if reading my mind.

Tears pricked my eyes, but I dared not blink. I swallowed hard and averted my eyes.

"The man who hurt you…" he said carefully, then

carried on without waiting for my answer. "Is he still alive?"

I'd have to reveal something if Jason was to continue pushing himself into my life. I had to reveal how the man I'd once loved had abused and hurt me. It was such a cliché story, but it's my story. I wanted to protect my body and my heart, and it would be easier to just push Jason away. I was far too young to be cynical and lead a solitary life. But I couldn't hide from were-animals all my life, especially now that I was becoming one.

Jason didn't push me for an answer, so we continued walking the rest of the way in silence. With my head against his shoulder, I closed my eyes and felt the vibrations of his breathing with each step. They were comforting and set me at ease. And he smelled so good; his fresh aftershave mixed with earthy undertones and a slight hint of his animal.

When he stopped walking and let go of me, I opened my eyes to find we had arrived at his shop. He opened the front door, switched on the lights and momentarily blinding me. Once I was inside, he locked the door behind me.

He pointed at a stool and said, "Sit there while I fix you a cappuccino."

For once I listened to him, sat on the chair and watched him make my coffee.

Jason

I almost fell asleep when something told me to look toward her apartment building doors. My heart stopped in my throat when I saw her standing there with a bright smile, and something else lingering in her twinkling eyes. I would've said she craved *something*, but I wasn't sure.

My overwhelming need to ensure her safety crushed my fluttering emotions, and I went to her side to ensure she was okay.

When I was sure the rogue wasn't near us, I relaxed. Then when Claire wanted me to come upstairs for coffee, I'd smelled a change in her. My body stirred with a growing desire. I'd love nothing more than to pleasure her with my body. But it was too soon. She was a tough nut to crack, and I didn't want to scare her off completely. I needed to go slowly with her, and if I went upstairs now; I didn't think I could control myself around her. Instead, I thought it best to go to my shop and make her coffee there. That way, she'd get to know me better instead of our relationship just being about the physical aspect.

At my coffee shop I ground the coffee beans, warmed the milk and my mouth salivated at the first smell of the coffee pouring into her mug. Since she was staying here and not rushing off to work, I didn't want to give her a takeaway cup. Instead, I gave her one of mine.

I handed her the warm mug. She brought it near her nose, closed her eyes and smelled the steam.

"I love the smell of your coffee first thing in the morning," she beamed. She opened her eyes and glanced at the mug in her hands. "Is this one of your mugs?"

"It is, since you aren't leaving soon, I thought you could do with decent crockery."

She guffawed, and the sound swirled around my heart, and I beamed at her.

"I'm just putting the muffins in," I said, glimpsing at the clock. I was an hour earlier than usual, but at least I had everything prepped in time for Sunday rush.

Once the muffins were baking, I made myself a

cup of coffee and sat across from her. The silence wasn't uncomfortable as we enjoyed our coffee.

As we sat there, each sipping from our mugs, I wanted to talk about her. But I wasn't sure whether to push the reason she had anger towards were-wolves or were-animals. Yet I had to understand more. It was the only way we could move forward. When I opened my mouth to ask my question again, she cut me off.

"I dated a were-wolf who hurt me," she said sadly.

Beast lifted his head from where he was resting in the metaphysical realm, snarling at her words. He didn't like that someone had hurt her, and neither did I.

'We must protect our female,' Beast said.

'What do you think I'm doing?' I thought back.

He growled at my comment.

'Sleep, I'm busy here.'

He harrumphed as much as a wolf could and lowered his head, but his ears remained pointed up, listening.

"His pack tried to help me, but not even they were a match for his flavor crazy. He tortured me for the last time when I killed him in self-defense. His pack helped keep me safe from his family and lied about how he died. I left seven months ago and came here." Her words were soft, but they held strength.

"Do you think they'll come after you?"

"No, only a handful of people know what happened. And they'll protect me. But," — she shrugged, — "somewhere along the line hate grew within me and against *all* were-animals. He was high within the pack ranks, and I'm reminded of him every day from the marks he left on my body." She touched her chest as she stared at me with pain in her eyes. As if her being slightly disfigured would be a deterrent for me. And I knew by sharing this with me was a tremendous step for her, one I appreciated. This was a secret from her past, and I'd never use it against her or get her into trouble. I wanted to protect this woman, and because of her trust in me, I'd do everything in my power to keep her safe.

I placed my mug on the counter and approached her. She set her mug on the counter, too. When I cupped her face and closed the gap she didn't pull away. Her mouth was inches away from mine, I felt her warm breath against my lips. She didn't push me away, and I took it as an invitation to kiss her.

Her lips were soft against mine as I teased them with my tongue. She opened her mouth and welcomed me inside, her tongue sweeping against mine. She tasted of coffee, as I was sure I did too.

Our kiss intensified when I pushed her legs apart with my leg, and she wrapped her arms around my waist, pulling me closer.

Her touch burned my skin through my shirt, and I welcomed the heated sensation. I felt alive in her embrace. I could only hope I did the same for her.

We bruised each other's lips like it was our first kiss in a long time; it most probably was. I drank every inch she offered, but I wanted more.

I pulled away because I didn't think she was ready for anything more than just a first kiss. Not yet. I pushed my beast down to ease his excitement, but it lingered, he wanted more of our female.

When I stepped back; her eyes were still closed and her hands bunched my shirt, not wanting to let go.

I bent down for a chaste kiss.

Claire opened her eyes and smiled. "That was nice," she said, licking her lips.

"It was," I said, and sat across from her again. I picked up my mug and enjoyed a long sip, not taking my eyes off her.

"And yes."

Confused by what she was saying *'yes'* to, I furrowed my brows and asked. "For what?"

"To your offer to help me with my change."

My smile broadened, and I nodded. "Good."

Claire

"Now that your fangs have already elongated," Jason said, sitting across from me at a table in his coffee shop. "Can you tell me if there's anything else strange happening to your body?" He whispered so that nobody else heard. He'd opened the doors when two of his baristas arrived, and then the shop quickly filled with customers.

"I'm not as nauseated as before," I said as I thought about his question. "This will sound strange, but I feel like I can breathe in more air. I feel stronger but I haven't tested it yet, but I know I can break a chair if I really wanted to," I grinned.

Jason's smile lit up his face.

"My fingernails and my joints tingle," I continued. "Oh, and I'm having dreams about running in the forest in my wolf if that makes any sense."

His eyebrows shot up. "Already? Those I've mentored showed signs of the change at a much slower rate... hmm," he considered me. "You're changing quickly, and I doubt you have to wait for the moon for your first change, although it might speed up the process during the change."

I nodded with a thin smile. I'd already dreamed he had told me that, so it wasn't a complete shock to my system. But what confused me was the dream itself. It was impossible for me to know these things, to dream of them, if we had never spoken about them before.

Although I'd dated a were-wolf, I didn't know much about their business or what was involved. My ex never included me in any of his business or spoke of such things.

"I've only heard of this happening to one of our wolves," he continued, bringing me out of my thoughts. "After his attack, his change occurred within the first week."

"Do you think I'll change in the first week, too?" I asked, rubbing my palm with my other hand. Suddenly my skin warmed all over and not just my face. This wasn't an embarrassed feeling, more like anticipating the worst.

"I don't know," he said seriously. "The shop isn't

open for long on Sundays. If you're up to it. We can take a drive and see if David is at home," he said deep in thought.

"Okay. I'd like that."

———

Around one o'clock Jason closed his shop, then completed his admin tasks. He said it was easier doing everything daily instead of at the end of the month. That way he monitored the stock even though he had an electronic system that reordered when supplies ran low. It was a way for him to keep an eye on things. Previously, an employee had stolen from him, and he'd only found out at the end of the month. This way he kept his employees honest and his finger on the pulse of his business.

"Why a coffee shop?" I asked once he pulled out into traffic. "I mean, you're an alpha were-wolf, you should be beating your chest with your fists, building traps, or doing something a little—"

"Manly?" he asked with an uncontrollable laugh. "I used to bake with my mother growing up and tried various coffees with my dad. And since then, I've loved coffee and baking. And I always wanted to own a business, so, I opened 'Alpha Coffee'. There isn't another like it and definitely nothing owned by a shifter." His grin was contagious, and I couldn't help but grin with him.

"Fair enough, and your muffins are delicious. But I thought you bought the dough, then just baked them daily."

"Once a week I mix the ingredients and only bake a certain amount each day. That way they're fresh and the patrons keep coming back daily," he said with a salacious wink and my cheeks heated. He'd probably said that because I was one of those patrons who kept coming back for his delicious muffins. My mouth watered—they were good muffins.

We rode the rest of the way in silence.

The road to David's house took us near the Wolf Pack clubhouse except we turned left onto a gravel road.

Jason parked near a wooden cabin, and before we opened our doors, the cabin door opened.

I froze in my seat when I saw the man.

Jason felt my uneasiness and touched my elbow, but I couldn't move. The one-eyed man saw me and bolted.

"Shit," Jason blurted. "No wonder I hadn't seen him the last two days." He cast a worried look my way, but I sat frozen in my seat. "I don't want to leave you here alone, but I don't want him getting away. Can you run?"

My eyes stung, but I nodded slowly, unable to find my voice.

Jason climbed out of the truck and came to my side, proffering his hand. I grabbed his hand, and he pulled me to his side. We ran together in the direction David had gone.

After every couple of steps, Jason coaxed me into running faster, and each time I pushed myself to my limits, and realized I was running faster. In all my life, I never ran so quickly. Growing up, I never took part in track events, and here I was at my absolute best. I was sure I could beat some of the best sprinters.

Jason scented the direction David had disappeared, and I tried the same. All I smelled were pines, leaves, brushes, kicked up dirt and water. All the elements of the forest swarmed me when I caught the smell of something else; sweat and fear. To me, fear had a strange sour stench. If I was David and had an alpha wolf on my tail, I'd be crapping myself too.

We stopped near a burrow big enough for a man to crawl inside. I glanced at Jason and he wasn't even out of breath while I struggled to take in air. My hair was knotty, and tears streaked my face. Not wanting to ruin the surprise and tell Jason how great I felt, instead I waited for his direction. There was a reason he'd stopped; the sour, sweaty smell was strongest here.

"David!" Jason commanded, his voice deep and forceful. I shivered at his powerful tone. "You attacked a woman on Friday night. I suggest you get out of that hole. Now!" Jason was typing on his cellphone while speaking, and I wondered who he was texting. Before I had a look at what he was typing, something moved inside the hole.

Jason noticed, pocketed his cellphone and his demeanor changed. His lips curled over his teeth as they elongated and his eyes glowed.

My arms pebbled and I swallowed dryly. I was afraid for David. Staring at Jason, I knew he would kill David; and quickly.

Reflexively I stepped behind Jason, which he encouraged by pressing against my hip until I was completely behind him and took my wrist to place against his stomach. I felt the hard ridges and dips of his muscles and pressed my cheek against his back; he felt warm and safe. I wrapped my other arm around his waist and clung to him.

David emerged out of the hole, his body covered in dirt, and raised his hands.

"I don't remember. If I attacked anyone, it was an accident," David said with a quiver in his voice. "I honestly don't know what happened. You must believe me, Jason. You know me. I would never hurt anyone, especially a defenseless female. All I remember is going to bed, then waking with an eye missing."

David lowered his hands, and the next moment he stormed Jason. His shoulder connected with Jason's abdomen and into my hands. I groaned as the men shoved into me. I fell to one side while Jason ensured they went the other way.

The men fell to the ground, fists flying and legs kicking. Jason smashed his fist into David's face, but not before connecting his knuckles with Jason's cheekbone. Both men spat blood, climbed to their feet and continued fighting.

David morphed into his half-beast form; his upper body looked similarly to the wolf I'd seen that night, and I scooted away from the action on my ass.

Jason followed suit and turned into his magnificent white wolf from my dream, and I was curious how I'd known he was a white wolf if I'd never seen him before.

With both men sporting enormous claws for gloves, they started swiping and clawing at each other. There was blood dripping and sounds of distress from each of them.

Noises of people running and then surrounding us. I didn't know who they were. They could be here to help David, or they were on our side.

The uneasiness I'd felt earlier returned, unsure of my safety with so many men around us.

I stood up and stepped behind a tree to hide myself when a large hand grabbed my elbow. I yelped and tried pulling out of his grasp, but he was too strong.

"Easy, Claire, it's okay. We're here to help," Shawn said.

When he said his name and I had the guts to look at him to make sure it was him, I relaxed and he let go.

"Enough!" Shawn boomed, and the men stopped fighting.

David wiped blood from his mouth and cheek while Jason stood sucking in deep breaths.

"David?" That one word a silent question for David to answer.

David's shoulders slumped, and he avoided eye contact. He slowly approached his alpha.

"You haven't been to the Wolf Pack in a few days. Care to elaborate?" Shawn asked in a tone that made me afraid for David.

"As I said to Jason, I don't remember attacking anyone, I swear," David said, his eyes flitting to me then back to Shawn. "I woke the next morning with my eye missing." He pointed to the eye patch.

Shawn narrowed his eyes. "Were you drinking again?"

David bowed his head lower.

"Were you at home?"

"Yes, I don't remember leaving. Then the next morning I woke with an eye gone, and no memory of what happened. When I heard about the emergency meeting and what the rogue wolf did, I couldn't attend like this," — he pointed at his eye, — "nobody would believe me."

If this was true. Then there was another wolf out there, sporting a missing eye. It's when I remembered more about the evening he attacked me.

"What color are your eyes when you change into your wolf?" I asked.

"They're blue," Shawn and David said at the same time.

"The one who attacked me had gray eyes with flecks of green." I squeezed my eyes shut and moved my hand as I recalled poking out his eye. "And I took his left eye." I wiggled my index and middle finger on my right hand, both nails much shorter since I'd chipped and broken them when I gouged out his eye. "Then it's a freaky coincidence that your left eye is also missing." Then I remembered Jason mentioning a picture of the rogue. "Does he even look like the picture?"

Jason pulled the picture out of his back pocket and opened it up. He held it against David's face.

"There are similarities, though," I said, pointing

at David's cheeks and jaw. They were eerily similar to the guy in the grainy picture. "Do you have wolf family?"

David swallowed hard and cursed under his breath when he glimpsed at the picture. "My cousin, Kevin. I was expecting him to visit for a few days but he hasn't shown up yet."

"Maybe he showed up and found you drunk on your ass again. It was a perfect opportunity to pin the attack on you by removing your eye," Shawn said, then added. "Your cousin is still out there. You should've come in, David. Then we could've at least known about your eye and treated you."

"I know, and I'm sorry." He turned to face Jason. "Sorry about fighting you, but you know, everybody runs when they think they're in trouble."

"It's okay." Jason slapped David's shoulder. "At least we know who we're looking for. And you can help us bring him in."

Claire

I joined Jason at the Wolf Pack. They brought David with us for Mel to check his wound and whether there was an infection in the areas that were still raw within the eye socket.

While that was happening, I walked with Jason outside so he could explain more about the Wolf Pack and if I joined them, where I might fit in.

If I decided I wanted to train with them, I could join the ranks, but I'd have to fight males to determine my place within the rank. Although fighting was never to the death, I could end up injured. I'd heal but still, the thought unnerved me. The only fight allowed to death was if I challenged Shawn for his title; which I wasn't interested in at all.

Being part of the ranks meant I'd have to take part in search and rescues, help where needed, and I would have to kill if necessary. Thoughts of having someone else's life in my hands didn't sit right with me, and I wondered what I'd do when I found David's cousin and whether I'd be able to hurt him as he had hurt me.

If I didn't join the ranks, I could remain a regular member and do nothing. But I still had to attend their monthly meeting when the moon was at its fullest. As Jason mentioned, this was when everyone burst into their animal and hunted together.

"I'm scared, Jason," I admitted to him and the surrounding nature. "I was hoping I could avoid changing, but I know I can't. Now that I'm here and you telling me everything about the pack and what you do, I'm afraid."

Jason pulled me into a hug. I wrapped my arms around his middle and pressed my cheek against his chest. His body heat comforting, and my nervousness dissolved into a puddle by my feet.

"I understand how daunting this must be for you, but you aren't alone. And thank you for trusting me enough to say that."

He pulled away, glancing down at me with smiling blue eyes. He closed the gap and kissed me as passionately as he did in his coffee shop. I melted into his embrace and was happy to stay here. When he broke the kiss, misery enveloped me once more. I felt better when I reached for his hand.

"There are a few paths we take when we hunt," he said, pointing at a well-used path leading deeper into the forest. "And we always go as one. We're all comfortable with our bodies." He winked. "I'm warning you that on your first night here there will be a lot of nakedness," he smirked.

I stiffened. It sounded like fun until he got to the naked part. I wasn't a prude, and I loved the human form, but I had an issue showing everyone the scars on my body.

He kissed the top of my head reassuringly. "You'll be fine." He reached for my hand, leading me back to the clubhouse.

Once inside, we found David sitting in Shawn's office. He nodded in greeting. "No infection," he said, pointing at his eye. "But Mel found bits of glass and cork embedded in the tissue. I'd been drinking that night," he said sadly. "Everybody knows I drink a lot and I'm wondering if it isn't just a freaky coincidence. That it wasn't Kevin who removed my eye, but I fell and stabbed myself in the eye with a bottle."

"You know how strange that sounds?" Jason said.

"I know, but life is stranger than fiction." David shrugged. "Anyway—"

"Right," Shawn boomed behind us. "The two wolves who went through your house phoned back. They said some strange things, David."

David sat upright in the chair while we stepped

out of Shawn's way. Jason pulled me to one side to sit on the couch near the wall.

"You have three broken bottles in your trash outside along with a damaged eye. Are you making your own moonshine again, David?" Shawn asked, and the air in the room pulsed with angry power. When David didn't answer, Shawn continued. "I've warned you once before about making your own alcohol. You're not allowed to do it."

My arms pebbled at Shawn's tone and wondered whether he was going to strike David.

"Your moonshine is awfully potent, and it drives you crazy for days. Remember the last time?" Silence filled the space between us, and I huddled closer to Jason. "You held a knife to your throat because you kept saying something crawled beneath your skin and if you didn't get it out, you would slice your neck open. And you made comments about trackers in our heads. It makes me wonder if you weren't paranoid on Friday night after drinking three bottles of that crap, then your eye became this foreign object you needed to remove," Shawn said, shaking his head.

I heard David swallow from where I sat. The air stiffened as I struggled for air. I glanced at Jason and he, too, struggled. Shawn was powerful. But this potent flavor swirling around us seemed dangerous, and I didn't want to be in the way of it going off.

"Shawn!" Jason interrupted the conversation. "Tone down, we're struggling to breathe."

Shawn sat back in his chair and closed his eyes. "Sorry," — he opened his eyes, — "it makes me angry."

"I'm sorry—"

"No more warnings, David," Shawn said gravely. "I've arranged your space. They will help you manage your stress, the death of your twin brother, and for you to gain the building blocks on how to move forward. You know I give chances to those in my pack, but this is your third one. I have to set a precedence and if you can't keep in line, you're out."

David wiped his face with his sleeve and nodded. "I'll do everything you need me to do. But please don't kick me out. This pack is all I have left."

"Good, ensure you stay in line."

"Yes," David said, staring at the floor.

"Mel will take you to the medical center for admission. You will remain there for ninety days. And you will do everything they tell you to do. I want you back here healthy and ready to fill the rank with your obedience and strength."

David continued thanking Shawn as he walked to the door and met Mel. She waved hello and slipped her arm through David's, taking him away.

"Wow, that's nice of you. Some alphas aren't as understanding of their pack members and would rather leave them in the pit," I said. "Or a fate much worse."

"We don't have a pit, nor do we punish our own unless it's warranted," Shawn said sternly. "I understand what he's going through, and I'd prefer not to punish him for the hand life dealt him. He's a good man, he just needs a nudge in the right direction." He steepled his fingers and stared at me. "Now about you..." He left his sentence hanging as if I had to answer without being asked a question.

Finally I said, "What about me?" I turned toward Jason, who was staring at Shawn. The two men stared at each other for a heartbeat; communicating silently with each other.

"Are you joining us?"

"Oh, ah, probably. That's if you'll have me." I shrugged.

Shawn slapped his desk, making me flinch.

Jason squeezed my hand.

"Good. And take your time in deciding where you want to go. We need females in the ranks, but that's up to you." He moved papers around on his desk as if silently alerting us to the fact that the conversation was over.

Jason stood, pulling me up with him.

Jason

Claire wanted to go home and rest. She offered to buy takeout for dinner and for me to join her. This time I did not decline.

We sat on the floor across from each other with the coffee table between us. She sat on a cushion while I sat directly on the floor.

We ate our burgers in silence. When she finished her burger, I had already eaten two.

The chemistry between us was thick enough to cut through and I knew she felt it too. She kept stealing glances my way, then quickly stared at something on the ground or picked at a nonexistent item on her pants. And every time she glanced away, her cheeks blossomed a healthy shade of red.

"Do you want a beer or some wine?" she asked nervously. "Sorry, I should've offered before we started eating, but I was famished and couldn't wait to dig in."

"I'll have a beer," I said, picking up the empty containers, and throwing them away while Claire fluttered around her kitchen for glasses out the cupboard, and beer and wine out the fridge.

When I washed my hands, I felt her gaze on me like a weight. When I turned around, she quickly glanced at the sugar bowl like it was more interesting. She seemed nervous about something. I couldn't help but smile.

When I dried my hands, she almost bumped into me. She mumbled sorry and grabbed the corkscrew out of the drawer and tried to open the bottle of wine, but her hands were shaking. I stood behind her and reached for her hands. She relaxed and didn't pull away. Instead, she allowed me to guide her as we opened the bottle of wine together.

Her skin was soft to the touch. Her hair smelled like citrus, and her breathing was ragged.

The heat from her back pulsated against my front, and my growing need for her only grew larger in my pants. And I was sure she felt my erection pressing against her ass.

She leaned back against me with her head on my chest. I let go of the wine bottle. My right hand cupped her jaw and tilted her head back without hurting her neck. She turned in my embrace, rocked onto her toes, and crashed her lips against mine.

Claire moaned in our kiss as her hands roamed over my body, I picked her up and set her on the counter beside her wine bottle.

She'd already opened the beer bottle; I reached for it and had a long sip. I picked up the bottle of wine and offered it to her. She took four large gulps and set it down hard. The impact caused some wine to splash on the counter.

No words were needed. We knew what we wanted even if we were a little nervous.

I moved between her legs as I pulled her ass forward so she could feel me.

"You can stop any time you want to, you're in control," I said, meaning every word. Claire had only given me the highlights of her story and how she had killed the wolf she had dated in self-defense. I didn't know the details about how he'd hurt her and would never press the issue. For now, I'd follow her lead until such time that she wanted me to control the situation; even then I wouldn't hurt her.

Her eyes glistened in the low light, and she nodded. "I'd prefer not to do it here, though." She pointed toward the bedroom.

I grabbed her ass as she clutched my shoulders, wrapping her legs around my waist, and I carried her to the bedroom. I gently set her down on the bed and removed my shirt. Her eyes danced across my body, which only added fuel to my already burning fire of desire.

Claire stopped me from unbuttoning my jeans, pushed my hands away as she undid them and pulled down my pants. My cock sprang free, making Claire gasp. She took me in her warm hands, lowering her lips to the tip and licked around the head. I grabbed her hair gently, in need of touching her while she devoured my steel member.

With the combination of her warm mouth and hands working up and down my length, I didn't think I'd last much longer. I stopped her before I came, and wanted to undress her. She stopped me from touching her shirt, and it felt as though I'd done something wrong.

"I'm sorry. Did I hurt you?" I asked nervously.

"No, you didn't hurt me, but I'd prefer to leave the shirt on," she said, her voice quivering.

"Whatever you need, babe," I said and leaned in to kiss her. "You can stop me anytime, okay." I repeated the words, so she understood I wouldn't be angry. I was not that guy. Her experience with me would be different.

I nudged her back onto the bed, removed her panties and settled between her legs. I licked, sucked, and teased her slick folds, tearing soft mewling sounds from Claire. When I inserted a finger, her eyes rolled into the back of her head as I continued licking. Then I inserted two fingers and started pumping my fingers inside of her until I found the rhythm that made her scream my name.

She clenched around my fingers as her first orgasm smashed into her. When I removed my fingers, sounds of disappointment echoed the room. I grinned. I wasn't done with her yet.

I moved above her with an elbow on either side of her head, my cock teasing her entrance. Claire lifted her hips, eager for me to sink myself into her. I moved my hips until I pressed right against her and thrusted the head inside. The sudden movement tore a gasp from Claire and her eyes shot open; her smiling blue eyes met mine and her pupils dilated.

I entered her heated sheath, working my way to the hilt and eased back out. I repeated the process, finding my rhythm.

Claire grabbed my ass, pulling me closer.

I felt the same; needing to feel more of her and to sink deep within her. I lifted her right leg over my elbow for a deeper reach and thrusted harder.

"Oh gods, yes," she moaned.

The sounds of our lovemaking filled the room, and my heart swelled with emotions I'd never felt before. I wasn't sure whether it could already be love, but it was damn close. I'd felt something similar to another, but not again. Whatever this was, it was all-consuming; my mind, my body, and my soul.

I watched Claire enjoy the rhythm of my body as we melded into one. Then, as if she felt my stare, she opened her eyes and reached for my face. We kissed with a fierceness that sent me overboard.

My heart warmed and my soul finally at ease at the thought of this beauty beneath me. I never wanted to let her go. She was the only one for me. She was mine, and even my wolf wanted her. I'd never possess her, as she would never possess me; but we were right for each other. All I had to do was show her my love and in time she would feel something for me, too.

I wanted to say, "*I love you*" in our kiss, but didn't want to scare her away. I'd leave that revelation for the right moment.

'*Good,*' thought Beast. '*I'll blame you for chasing our female away.*'

'*Shhh, I'm busy here.*'

Claire cried out as her orgasm smashed into her, which fueled my release. I relished in the fact that I made those sounds come out of her and slowed my motion as the rippling waves of carnal passion eased. I loved the feel of being inside her as she continued contracting around me.

I kissed her once more before pulling out and lay

beside her. Claire wanted to move away from me, but I pulled her closer and kissed her temple.

"There's no running away from me, Claire. I'm here to stay and won't hurt you. Unless you want me to spank your ass. That's kinda kinky."

I heard her choke on a sob as she tried to laugh. I sat up on my elbow and reached for her face. With my thumb and index finger, I gently gripped her chin and pulled her face toward me.

"Are you laughing or crying? Did I hurt you?"

"No," she cried and laughed. "It's… it's just that," she swallowed. "It was beautiful. I've slept with Erik after, you know, but it was never this intense. You made it different. I've never felt a connection like this before. And you made my release more than just—"

"I care for you, Claire," — I kissed her again. My heart swelled with love for her, knowing I was the one who did it for her, — "and that's just the beginning. Do you want that spank now or later?" I joked, trying to make her smile and succeeding.

She laughed as she wiped her eyes dry. Then she pulled me closer for another chaste kiss.

"I don't think we're at spanking level yet, but thanks for the offer," she said, stifling another laugh.

I couldn't help it. My hand traveled down the side of her body. "Fair enough," — my hand settled on the tender skin near her waist, — "are we at least at the tickling stage?" I asked and attacked her waist with my fingers, finding the spot that drove her crazy.

She snorted, then laughed as she tried to swat my hand away. But I was far stronger than her, and I'd only use my strength to make her smile.

Claire

I woke the same time I did every day. The only difference was the warm body beside me. Erik never stayed over; he preferred to sleep in his own bed.

I used the bathroom and called Blaire. It relieved her to hear I was okay and was ecstatic to hear Jason was holding my hand through the process—if only she knew what else he'd been holding. She said I should stay at home for a few days. Since she and Ralph were away on a case, she doubted there'd be anything for me to do apart from the usual admin, and that could wait a few days. My health came first and she ordered me to rest. But I couldn't sit at home and watch TV all day, I'd go nuts.

When I came back to bed, Jason had the pillow

tucked beneath his head, on his stomach, and fast asleep. Resting my arm over his broad shoulders and my head against his back, I felt the rumblings of his breathing reverberate through my body.

Jason shifted onto his back, but continued holding me against him until I nestled against his side. He kissed my temple and mumbled, "Good morning, gorgeous."

"Uh, aren't you going to be late to open your shop?"

"What time is it?"

"Almost seven."

"Yes," he smiled, sitting up. "Are you working today?"

"Nah, I just got off the phone with Blaire. She said to chill at home, but I can't stay here all day and for the week."

"You're welcome to come in with me if you like." He winked and kissed me chastely. He climbed out of bed and sauntered toward the bathroom. "I hope you don't mind me using your shower. And you're welcome to join me if you like."

My heart stuttered thinking about stripping completely naked for him, but I couldn't, not yet. "No, it's fine. I'll shower after you."

"Okay, your loss," he teased, and slapped his left ass cheek.

I smiled, even though he couldn't see it. He made me happy. My walls were still up, but he was tearing them down brick by brick.

I'd show him the scars one day, but not today.

———

We arrived at Jason's coffee shop with a minute to spare. Two of his baristas were already waiting for him, casting side glances my way. I brushed it off as I followed Jason inside, his hand enveloping mine.

I helped with the muffins while the two employees started with the first orders. Although the muffins would be late, Jason had some leftover from yesterday which he warmed up for customers who couldn't wait.

The kitchen was as small as the one in my place. Jason had said he didn't want to extend it since he preferred it small. It reminded him of his mom's kitchen, and it was easier moving around. He didn't have a dishwasher and washed his own dishes. I said I'd help since he didn't have time to do it yesterday.

Jason rolled his sleeves up to his elbows. He was positively delicious as he washed dishes while I dried and packed them away.

I watched the corded muscles on his forearms work to clean the six muffin pans, cutlery and crockery. He seemed content doing a chore usually reserved for women. I could tell he took pride in his coffee shop and everything within.

As I dried one pan, Jason flicked soap suds at me, hitting the side of my face. I flinched, wiped my face dry and flicked the dishtowel at him, striking his ass. He growled low. His eyes glowed yellow, leaving me in a quivering puddle. I squirmed out of his arms as he tried to tickle me.

A barista entered the kitchen and shushed us. We stood side by side like naughty school kids caught with our hands in the cookie jar. When the barista left, he smacked my ass.

"Payback." He chuckled lightheartedly and continued washing.

Not wanting to admit it out loud, but I had fun with Jason in his coffee shop. We laughed and joked with each other while hiding out in the kitchen. He showed me how he managed things, and I helped him prepare the muffins for the week since he'd used the last batch that morning. Then when it was time to add the secret ingredient, he whispered it to me; "*An extra dash of vanilla essence, and to use butter and oil to make them moist.*"

My mouth watered at the smell of the first batch baking.

The rest of the day flew by. I sat at a corner table with a cappuccino in one of Jason's mugs and read a magazine until after lunch. Jason had ordered a chicken salad for me while he ate a meaty dish. He left me at the table while he finished up on some business.

After I'd eaten, I watched the passersby on the sidewalk; some had been shopping, while others rushed back to work.

My stomach tightened. Bile rose, and I swallowed hard. Ice filled my veins, and a shudder ran through me. I carefully set my mug on the table and stood slowly. Not wanting to throw up where I sat or near customers, I walked slowly yet at a brisk pace toward the bathroom. Sweat dripped down the sides of my face as I struggled to open the door. One barista noticed and aided me by opening the door.

"Do you need any help?" she asked.

I pursed my lips and shook my head.

I darted for the open cubicle, slamming the door closed behind me. My arms throbbed as my stomach pained. Watching in horror as my hands shifted into dark claws as volts of electricity coursed through my veins. I didn't realize I was screaming until Jason banged on the door, which opened, hitting me in the back.

"It's okay, come here," he breathed, reaching for

my hands. He entered the cubicle with me and locked the door.

"Help me," I cried, and doubled over again.

"It's going to be okay. It's the gene working its way through your system and needing you to change. You need to allow it. The more you fight it, the worse the pain gets." He closed the toilet seat lid and sat down, pulling me onto his lap. "First, you need to steady your breathing." He sucked in air and I did the same. "And try to calm down. I know it's the worst thing to say to someone panicked, but try," he added.

I closed my eyes as I listened to Jason voice and his breathing. The whir of the air conditioner above us caught my attention, along with a faucet dripping water.

My heart hammered in my chest as sparkly stars flashed behind my eyelids.

I breathed in time with Jason as he rubbed my arms; the sensation of his touch distracting me. The pain ebbed and my fingers tingled. I fisted my hands and they felt tight, my skin pulling, then slowly I relaxed them.

My hands heated, the tingling receded. When I opened my eyes, my hands were back to normal.

Jason wiped sweat from my forehead and cradled me in his arms. "Are you feeling better?"

"Uh-huh, thanks," I said and leaned into him. It

was so comforting to be near him. The heat from his body like a warm blanket and his caring nature enduring. I didn't want to move away from him.

"When that happens again, call me and I'll help you through the change." He kissed my temple and stood with me still in his arms. "Your body is going to continue like this until you change into your wolf. At the rate you're going, it will be soon. I'm thinking you should join me in the coffee shop every day until you shift?"

"I'm going to scare your customers away."

He chuckled. "Doubtful, they know a were-wolf owns the place. I think they expect action once in a while," he smiled sweetly.

"Did your barista tell you I was in trouble?"

"No," — he shook his head, — "I felt something was wrong. When I didn't see you sitting at the table, I thought you might be here."

"Thank you."

Jason carefully set me down onto shaky legs, but I continued to use him as a walking aid. I didn't know how long I'd been in the bathroom. When we exited, the shop was already empty.

"Luckily you close your shop early."

"Yep, and I don't want to leave you alone in your apartment this afternoon. Come with me to the Wolf Pack. When I'm done with business, we can come to your apartment again. But after I grab fresh clothing from home."

I beamed at him. Another brick just fell as he continued chiseling at my wall with his kindness. If he kept this up, the wall around my heart might fall completely.

Claire

We locked up *Alpha Coffee* and headed to the Wolf Pack. Jason had a daily meeting to discuss important items, but their primary focus was finding the rogue, David's cousin, Kevin, who was still out there somewhere.

Mel phoned Jason on his cellphone to let him know David had arrived safely at the center to start his recovery.

From what I gathered from Jason's conversation with Mel, Shawn and other were-animals still needed a plan to apprehend the rogue before he hurt someone else.

We arrived at the clubhouse in chaos. People running around shouting words that left me stunned.

Kevin had attacked someone else, only they

weren't as lucky. In the early hours of the morning, a woman was on her way to work when the rogue attacked her. The security camera near one of the shops recorded the attack. With the help of the police, a Detective Georgina Carson, had agreed to work with us in Blaire's absence. From prior cases Blaire had told me she worked closely with Georgina and was one of the few cops we could trust.

Jason didn't want to leave me alone, so I accompanied him to Shawn's office, where there were other high-ranking alphas. The energy within the room knocked the breath right out of me, forcing me to lean against the wall or I'd collapse. Jason pulled me toward him as he sat on the nearest chair, and I sat on his lap. The power within the room subsided slightly, but not much. My arms still pebbled.

Shawn raised his eyebrows when he saw I was there, then his eyes flitted between Jason and me but said nothing.

"By now you've heard what had happened," Shawn said sternly.

Everybody nodded and mumbled, "Yes."

"Georgina has allocated two officers to help track down Kevin. From the video, it's apparent Kevin's injured. He limped toward the unsuspecting female and attacked her. She managed a few good kicks to his groin before he clawed at her throat. Unfortunately, she succumbed to her injuries before emergency services could respond. Troy has indicated one of his lions may have found someone matching Kevin's description. He limped into a restroom near the park and hasn't exited yet. I've sent five of our best wolves to wait with the lions, and they have instructed everybody to bring the rogue here."

I flinched when Shawn smashed his fist into his desk, splintering it as wood clippings flew. The veins in his neck bulged, his skin reddened, and his eyes glowed yellow before settling back to their usual cool-blue. I thought he was going to shift into his beast, tapering down his anger.

Jason squeezed my waist for reassurance.

When everybody filed out of the office with their various tasks, we remained behind.

Shawn peered at us as if to ask, *'what do you want?'*

"Kevin is ours when they bring him in?" Jason asked.

"Absolutely, and Claire is more than welcome to kill him if she wants. Otherwise, I'll leave it to you, Jason."

"Thanks," Jason said, lifting me to my feet as he stood. "We'll wait in the dungeon."

———

We didn't have to wait long.

They caught Kevin the moment he exited the public restrooms. He didn't have time to think about what was happening when five men pounced on him.

Jason had told me there were about fifty men from various shifter groups surrounding the restrooms near the park where he'd attacked me. They ensured Kevin had no way of escaping and secured him in unbreakable shackles and a blindfold.

My palms were clammy and sweat dripped down the middle of my back. Just thinking about seeing Kevin again left me in a bundle of nerves. I tried to block out his face, but it seemed my mind had other plans. I recalled that night, the feeling of being watched and then stalked. Then sounds of his growl surrounding me in that ominous park.

I swallowed hard as I remembered the attack and the feeling of his firm jaw sinking into my tender flesh, followed by the pain. So much pain.

Instinctively, I reached for my forearm.

Then I remembered his enormous claws tearing through my skin. Visions of his muzzled face close to mine left me breathing heavily, and my chest squeezed.

"Are you okay?" Jason asked with concern etched in his face.

I nodded, not trusting myself to speak. I needed to calm down first.

Footsteps echoed down the stairs toward the dungeon where we waited. The walls of the large room were lined with were-wolves standing shoulder to shoulder with hardly any space in-between. Everyone was here. Everyone wanted to witness the rogue's demise.

The four walls seemed to close in on me as the footsteps neared. I counted at least ten pairs of boots hitting the steps with one dragging a chain.

I squeezed Jason's hand when their shadows reached the doorjamb. My eyes raked up the body of the man shackled, and I froze when his one grey eye penetrated mine. I felt his dark gaze as recognition registered in his mind. He knew who I was. The moment his lips stretched into an enormous smile; my cheeks heated with anger. I clenched my hands into fists and stars danced before my eyes as rage filled my veins.

I wanted Kevin to hurt as much as he had hurt me. To have him bound and bleeding for what he'd done. He'd bitten me—almost killed me—and turned me into a creature of the night. It was something I never wanted. He had removed all choices from me and I needed him to hurt.

Jason patted my hand, breaking my concentration, and I turned to look at him. He smiled lovingly.

His crystal blue eyes calming me. He gently thumbed my cheek, then cupped my face as he brought me closer, kissing me. His lips were soft against mine and it wasn't a normal kiss, it was a kiss filled with love and every wonderful emotion. I felt every part of his soul in that kiss.

"I can hear your teeth grinding," he said with kindness. "Don't hurt yourself over him, it's not worth it."

I didn't realize I was doing that and stretched out my jaw. My jaw muscles ached when I relaxed them and noted I'd been grinding my teeth for some time. I massaged along my jawline and felt better.

"Thanks," I said, leaning into Jason. With my face near his ear, the smell of him calmed me. My anger washed away. I couldn't understand how he grounded me, but he did. I reached for his hand and settled it on my lap while I held onto him with both hands.

I wanted revenge for what Kevin had done to me, but would I feel better? Would his death ease the pain I suffered? These were questions I didn't know the answer to.

Perhaps I had to forgive and move forward with my life.

Or perhaps Shawn and his wolves could do with Kevin as they pleased. Their revenge might be enough for me to move forward. But Kevin had stripped away my humanity by turning me into something I despised. By attacking me, Kevin had not only hurt me, scared me, but damaged me for the rest of my life.

My ex had hurt me, but he was always careful not to infect me.

But Kevin was something else, something scarier.

I understood that by turning into a were-wolf, I would become stronger and live longer than if I were human. The outcome of the attack was great, and I now had Jason in my life. Who knew what I would've done if nothing had happened and I'd continue pushing Jason to one side.

I exhaled a confused breath as thoughts crashed one into the other until my head hurt. I didn't know what to do.

Staring at my open hands with Jason's larger hand on my lap, I couldn't imagine blood on them. That's what I had to do; to hurt Kevin using my hands.

I didn't know if I could do it. Even after all the stuff I'd gone through with my absent parents, the relative who'd left me at the church, or my ex who'd abused me. All those wrongs didn't mean I had to do the same to make things right.

I squeezed Jason's hand. There was only one thing to do.

Claire

They fastened Kevin's shackles to a metal chair bolted to the floor.

The air inside the dungeon was thick and stuffy, the smell of animal and hints of sweat lingering.

Shawn stepped forward. "Kevin, we accuse you of murder and assault. How do you plead?"

Kevin didn't answer. Instead, he threw his head back and cackled. His one eye never leaving mine. His lips curled as he snarled, and his face shifted into his wolf. Before he changed completely with the possibility of breaking his chains, someone injected him with something, and he morphed back into human form.

"What's that?" I whispered into Jason's ear.

"It's a serum to stop the change. It's temporary

though, with the potency to kill. I'd advise against using it to try to stop your change. We do, however, use it down here only," he said, his tone ominous as he stared daggers at Kevin. His hand caressed my thigh tenderly.

"Claire," Shawn said. "He is yours to do with as you please."

Nodding, I stood up from my safe seat and approached. I had to do this; I had to understand why. My body shook with anger. The closer I stepped toward Kevin, and with Jason at my back, I realized there were things I couldn't do—not yet, anyway. And the moment I did them, I could never undo them. It would be a point of no return and I wasn't in a hurry to get there.

I stood inches away from Kevin. He seemed small and fragile, but knew he wasn't. I had to know why. "Why did you attack me, and why did you kill that woman?"

One corner of his mouth tilted upward. "Why not? Something as delicious as you all alone in the dark park..." he purred. "Who wouldn't?" he sneered. "I took one look at you and knew I had to taste you." Before he had first spoken in a Southern accent, then it shifted back to something similar to someone from Boston.

The change threw me off guard, and I didn't know what to say. I took my time in replying and finally said. "You killed a woman!" I raised my voice. "She did nothing to you and you've infected me. You've ruined lives."

His shoulders dropped, and his demeanor changed. He rolled his shoulders and moved his head from side to side like one would before a fight.

"Why must everything have a reason?" he finally said. "I like to play. And you, pretty thing, you were alone in the park. At night. Didn't anyone ever tell you it's dangerous?" he smirked and said *'dangerous'* in a Southern accent. "I was hungry and if you weren't so feisty, I would've done a lot more to you." He slowly licked his lips as his one eye raked up my body.

I shuddered as I imagined the vile thoughts going through his head. My body heated at what he could've done to me; flashes of him having his way with me only fueled my anger. My hands balled into fists until my fingernails punctured the skin.

Jason placed calm hands on my shoulders and rubbed the stiff muscles.

No matter what Kevin said that pushed my buttons, I wouldn't lower myself to his standards. He was nothing—he was less than nothing. He was an evil creature who preyed on the vulnerable and would never amount to anything.

Except... What happened next was a reflex. I knew I couldn't kill him, but I had to do something to expel the frustration within. I slapped him across his face so hard I left red welts and my hand stung.

Kevin burst out laughing. The maniacal, high-pitched laughter like blades down my back. "Ooh, yeah, baby. I love it when they fight back." His grin was back. His teeth colored red. He smacked his lips together and licked the drops of blood. "It doesn't matter what you do to me, you'll always remember what I did to you. Have you changed yet, darlin'?" He giggled. "I'd love to know the color of your fur when you change. You aren't the first, you know. Everywhere I've been, I've blessed a woman with my gift. Sometimes it was pleasurable for her, but it was always pleasurable for me. I've made them part of something bigger than they'll ever know," he shouted, ensuring everybody heard him. It reminded me of a sermon. "I helped make our family larger." He cackled again. "And darlin', I wish I had more time with you!" He yelled the word 'you', making me flinch and step backward into Jason.

I made a mental note about Kevin's confession assaulting other women. I wasn't sure of the protocol and wanted to know whether we alerted the police to such confessions or if we dealt with it ourselves.

I turned to face Jason with tears in my eyes. I knew I shouldn't show my back to a killer, but I couldn't face him anymore. "Please deal with him however you deem fit. I can't," I whispered near the shell of his ear and wiped my eyes.

Jason kissed my temple, never taking his eyes off Kevin, and gently moved me behind him.

"Oh, that's what I'm talking about," Kevin said with a sinister laugh. "I do enjoy a man's company, darlin'; the more the merrier; the bigger the better. Are you the one to make me pay?" He cackled.

I turned around in time to see Jason slam his fist into Kevin's face, snapping his head backward. I thought he broke his neck, but Kevin just continued laughing. The chair creaked as the metal bolts in the floor moved.

Jason hit him again and the chair legs broke free from the bolts on the floor, causing Kevin to fall backward. A crowd of were-wolves surrounded Kevin in case he escaped his shackles, but he wasn't moving. He wasn't even laughing.

Jason jumped onto Kevin's body, straddling his chest, and smashed his fists into his face one after the other until his head caved. Blood pooled everywhere, and the front of Jason's shirt stained red.

Other wolves tore Jason from Kevin's lifeless body, or he'd smash his fists into the floor.

Jason

I didn't want Claire to see the destruction and potent violence raging within me. It's one reason Shawn had me high in the ranks—my fighting ability. It was better to have me as an ally than an enemy. But I would never go after his position as alpha; he was strategic in his actions whereas I preferred to use my fists.

That's the reason I had my coffee shop; baking was therapeutic for me and cheaper than therapy. It calmed my soul, but occasionally I let loose. And Kevin received my deserving wrath.

I climbed off Kevin's corpse, yanking my arms free of the other wolves. The front of my shirt and face dripped with his blood. I could only imagine how horrific I looked. But when I turned to face Claire, I braced myself for a disappointing look.

Instead, she ran toward me with concern etched on her beautiful face and reached for my hands.

"You're bleeding," she said, staring at my knuckles. Then she pulled me to one of the unisex bathrooms. "And your shirt is full of his blood. Take it off," she shrieked.

She didn't wait for me to respond and reached for the hem of my shirt, pulling it over my head, careful not to let the wet parts touch my face. Then she grabbed pieces of toilet paper and wiped most of the blood off my face, then using the clean parts of my shirt to wipe the blood off my arms. Then with a tender touch she washed my hands, careful not to hurt me.

"The wounds will heal by tomorrow," I whispered, needing to let her know it was fine. She didn't have to fret over me.

"I must wash his tainted blood off of you. Now! I can't have him stain you, too," she said as she continued scrubbing my hands with soap and water.

When my hands were clean, I told her to stop. But she didn't. Claire continued washing as if still marked with his blood. When I grabbed her hands, she stilled, then her body jerked as the tears fell.

"Come here," I said, turning her around and bringing her closer. I held her as she cried. I caressed her head and shoulders and kissed her temple every few seconds until her body stilled.

I waited until Claire was ready. She let go first and reached for the toilet paper again, tore off a few pieces, wiped her face and blew her nose. Her blue, red-rimmed eyes seemed translucent from the tears she shed. She looked better and even forced a smile.

"Are you feeling better?" I asked carefully. She'd just witnessed me brutally smash a man's face in—a man who had attacked her, which resulted in her life changing forever. A lot had happened in only a short number of days. Everything had most likely caught up with her, and I needed to be patient. I needed to be there for her.

"Yes." She nodded, but tears still pricked her eyes.

"How about we go home?" I asked.

"I'd like that."

I reached for her hand and pulled her close to my side. We greeted everyone, and Shawn nodded curtly.

Claire had gone through enough. I didn't want to hang around while they disposed of Kevin's body.

————

We stopped outside my place first to grab a couple of items before we headed to her apartment.

She came inside with me and approved of my place with all the *'ooh's'* and *'aah's'*.

"Your place is nice."

"Thanks," I said. "Give me a minute to grab a few things, then we can go."

"Okay." She entered each room as she followed me to the main bedroom. "How long have you had your house?"

"A few years."

"Don't you think it's a bit big for only one man?"

"I bought it when I asked my girlfriend to marry me. We wanted lots of children and this house was perfect."

She gasped and covered her mouth. "What happened? Why aren't you married with kids?" She fell silent, then added. "You don't have to tell me if it's too painful."

"No, I will tell you everything you want to know." I grabbed a duffel bag from my closet and added a couple of shirts, pants, underwear, and socks. "I thought she was the one, you know. We married, she fell pregnant. Everything was going perfectly. Then she was in a car accident." I shrugged. It didn't hurt to say the words, not anymore.

"Oh, Jason, I'm so sorry. I didn't know."

"It happened ten years ago. I've worked through the pain and emotions that came with it. And I'm ready to move on." I zipped the duffel closed, slung the strap over my shoulder, and stopped in front of her, rubbing her arms. "You're cold. Let's go."

She pulled her face into a questioning look as if there was more to the story.

"And you never wanted to date again?" she asked carefully.

"No." I shook my head. "I had one-night stands but nothing serious. I needed time to heal, otherwise the next relationship wouldn't last. I'm very particular about my choices and she has to be worth it." My smile reached my eyes.

Tears welled in her glacier-blue eyes again. I cupped her face and kissed her with my everything; my heart and my soul.

"And you, Claire, are worth it."

Claire

I kept stealing glances at Jason as he drove us to my apartment. What he did for me at the Wolf Pack by destroying Kevin's face should have scared me to death. It was violent and an awful way to die. I couldn't imagine what Kevin was going through, but glad it happened. It made me elated that Kevin had suffered.

Was I sick thinking these thoughts, or was it justified? I was going with justified, but wondered whether Jason's soul was now tainted or if it already was before he killed Kevin.

Then my heart broke when I saw his enormous house. He had five bedrooms, and I suspected he and his wife had wanted at least four children. It surprised me that after ten years he hadn't remarried.

And from the sounds of it, he hadn't bothered dating anyone seriously until he met me.

I wanted to cry again when he said I was worth it. That he waited for someone like me to come into his life. I was nobody with no family. Yet he had defended me by destroying the man who'd attacked me.

I flinched when his hand covered mine and he squeezed tenderly. I hadn't realized I was daydreaming, but when he touched me, my hands were clammy, and they felt raw.

"You seem tense, again."

"I'm just thinking about everything that happened," I said as I stared out the car window. I watched the streetlights blur past. Rain had fallen, but it didn't last long, just enough to make the streets shine under the lights.

We drove the rest of the way in silence, which continued when we arrived at my apartment.

I walked into my apartment, stopping in the middle of the living area while Jason locked the door.

I felt lost in the moment. I felt drained and exhausted. All I wanted to do was sleep.

"Are you okay?" he asked carefully and approached slowly.

I nodded mechanically, without glancing at him.

"Come here." Jason reached for my hand and pulled me closer.

I turned toward Jason. He was still bare chested with smears of blood everywhere. His skin glowed with sweat, and although he looked like a dangerous street fighter, his kind smile brought me out of my depressing funk. While his tender touch made my skin tingle.

My core heated as my body came alive. It was then I realized I had to stop thinking about the past and look to my future; with Jason. He was standing with me, here and now. What had happened in the past was over, and I needed to move forward with my new life. And here was this were-man who didn't stop in his pursuit of my affection. The least I could do was reciprocate.

I was suddenly wide awake.

"Let's shower," he said, reaching for my hand and leading the way. He threw his duffle bag in my room and we entered the bathroom.

Without saying a word, he lifted my shirt above my head, leaving me in my bra. I wanted to protest, to stop him from seeing my scars. I felt ashamed for having them, even though I knew they weren't my fault. But I didn't stop him. I didn't turn away. He had shown me everything there was to know about him. I could do the same and allow him to see *me*.

Jason didn't show his disgust for my disfigured skin, nor did he run away. Instead, he kissed my neck as I clung to his shoulders. Then he kissed the scars on and between my breasts as he unclasped the bra. He hissed when my breasts spilled free, grinning like a naughty boy.

Next he unbuttoned my jeans, removed my shoes and socks, then slipped the jeans and panties off in one go.

He removed his shoes, socks, and pants in one swift motion.

We stared at each other. Totally naked; each vulnerable to the other. No clothing to hide behind. No reason to feel shame. We were completely available to the other.

His gaze raked up and down my body, and a low rumbling growl escaped his lips.

"If the man who did that to you was still alive. I'd kill him." He vowed.

I smiled sadly. Jason had been nothing but kind to me and did everything he could to set me at ease. He was my protector, my confidant, and my great love. The revelation caught me off guard, but it felt right. This was right.

"I love you." I jumped into his arms and kissed him with a fiery passion I'd never experienced.

His kisses were warm and gentle, a far cry from the violence I'd witnessed before. But he'd never hurt me. I knew that to be true.

"I love you, too," he said in our kiss. "Now let's shower so I can kiss every inch of your body."

Jason set the water at a warm temperature. It was heaven sent as the water washed the remnants of the day away, a day I'd gladly forget.

From this moment forward, it would just be the two of us.

Once we were both thoroughly wet, he added shampoo to his hands and told me to turn around. He washed my hair, massaged my scalp, and goosebumps flooded my body. I relaxed in his touch, enjoying his attention. He continued to wash my body, caressing the soft curves, then nipped my nipples as he massaged my ass. The feeling was absolutely divine.

When it was my turn, I washed his chest since I couldn't reach his head and then I washed lower. Moans of pleasure escaped his mouth, his eyes closed as he enjoyed my caresses. I stroked his hard member and balls then bent down, lowering my mouth to the tip, where I licked the pre-come to taste him; salty, slightly musky—*him*.

I continued stroking slowly up and down as my mouth covered him. Then he pulled me off.

"I'm going to finish if you don't stop." He kissed me and turned me around.

With my palms flat on the tiled wall, he entered me from behind. Jason gripped my hips and pushed deeper. The feel of him stretching me felt wonderful.

He found his rhythm as he pumped into me. His

hips moving back and forth as his thick, pulsing length continued sliding in and out of me.

My core contracted in satisfaction as my insides turned to a puddle of pleasure. Molten ecstasy exploded throughout my body, causing moans to escape my lips as I braced myself against the tiles.

My sounds triggered Jason's release, and his heated seed flooded my core, sending another wave of pleasure rippling through me.

We cleaned ourselves again and climbed out the shower.

By the time we were dry and in bed, it was midnight. Exhaustion took over as we clung to each other's naked body, our steady breathing helping us fall asleep.

Claire

I awoke with a burning pain throughout my body, gasping for air and someone holding me down. I opened my eyes to find Jason straddling my waist and pinning my hands above my head.

"You can let me go now." I squirmed to get away, but he didn't budge. "Jason? You can let go." I fought to get out of his stronghold, but he held tighter. "Jason!?" I yelled, but it didn't deter him.

I stared at the man restraining me, but instead of seeing Jason's handsome face, the hollow eye socket came into view, and I screamed.

"It's okay," said the faint voice. "I'm here," Jason said in a soothing tone, caressing my face, and pulling me into the curve of his warm body.

I opened my eyes to sun streaming into my room

and Jason comforting me. I turned around and squashed my face to his chest. "I dreamed Kevin was holding me down—"

My sentence was cut short when Jason's cellphone rang. "Let me get that quickly. It's the ringtone I've set for Mel. When she phones, it's usually serious."

"Hey?" Jason said. "Yeah, she's with me. Okay… uh… oh…" I only heard his side of the conversation. "Uh-huh." He nodded, his chin touching the top of my head. "Cheers."

Jason set his cellphone on the side table and glanced down at me. "When I brought you to Mel after your attack, she took samples of the white stuff oozing out of your wounds and had it tested. She gave me the results now." He moved, patting my arm. "We need to dress and get to the Wolf Pack now," he said gravely.

"Why? What's wrong?" When he didn't answer me, I added, "You're scaring me."

He stopped moving and glanced back at me. "Before I say what it is, understand it's not a common thing, but it's not serious either. Try to relax." He sat on the bed again and rubbed my shoulder as if that would sooth me. It didn't. I still felt tense. "Mel is going to try something to flush it out of your system. She'll take another blood sample before you start treatment and then take it from there."

"Okay, so what is it."

"It's a were-animal form of rabies."

"Rabies!" I yelled and bolted upright, not bothered by my nakedness. "I'm going to die."

"You won't die—"

"Or go mad. Maybe that's why Kevin acted so strange." I felt my eyes widen as my skin chilled yet remained hot.

"It could explain why you're changing so quickly. The wolf gene is trying to rid the virus."

I bolted out of bed and pulled on underwear and clothing. "Come. I want this sorted out now," I growled as panic settled into my bones, and my hands started shaking.

I hadn't seen Jason move, but he was already by my side and holding my hands. "It's going to be okay. This has happened before. Remember I said that David might have something similar to you. I'm thinking Kevin was the one who bit him, too. That means Kevin has had rabies for years. And David has been a wolf for at least thirteen years."

"Yeah, look how that turned out for him. He made his own alcohol, drank it, and stabbed himself in the face, removing an eye. I don't want to go crazy, Jason. So don't patronize me and let's go."

Jason said nothing else. He pulled clean clothing out of his duffle bag and dressed.

———

We met Mel at the Wolf Pack and followed her to the same room she treated me in before. She closed the door behind us and patted the bed.

"Hop on," she said with a warm smile.

Since I wasn't half dying and my vision clear, I finally saw what Mel looked like. Her big brown eyes held secrets I could only imagine, and her silver/gray hair cascaded over her shoulders. She was slightly shorter than me and well-built for her age; crow's feet in the corners of her eyes, with fine lines outlining her mouth when she smiled. Other than that, she seemed younger, with many years' experience.

"You look better than last time," she said, her tone kind, as she tested a vein in my arm. "I hope Jason told you why you're here?" I nodded. "Good, I'm just going to draw some blood to test, then I'm going to insert an IV drip with a solution to flush the virus from your system. It will work, so don't stress about getting sick. And we're only doing this now, so we don't have to worry about it later. It's still early days and I suspect there's no damage. But I'd rather be sure."

When Mel was happy with the one bulging vein, she inserted the needle and filled tubes with my blood. She worked carefully, and I hardly felt anything.

She packaged the tubes in a bag, marked them with my name, then returned with an IV filled with a strange orange/brown solution.

"This will prick, and you'll feel your arm getting cold, but it will settle."

She pushed the needle in, and I barely felt it, then the solution coursed through my veins. I shuddered at the chill, but it soon dissipated.

Jason stood beside me, holding my free hand.

Mel glanced between us and sniffed the air. She arched an eyebrow with a silent question.

"Yes, we're together," Jason said with an enormous grin.

"I'm happy for you." Her frown turned into a genuine smile, and she patted my thigh. "He's a catch and I'm glad to see him finally getting out there again." She squeezed Jason's shoulder. "Are you going to solidify the bond?"

"We haven't—" I wanted to say bonded, but in some strange way we had. We had sex, and we liked each other... but I wasn't sure whether Jason wanted to bind himself to me forever. I didn't think we were at that point.

"No," — Jason shook his head, — "not yet," he smiled slyly, and I raised both eyebrows.

"What do you mean '*not yet*'?"

"I mean, we haven't discussed it, but it's something I'd like."

"You didn't bond with your wife?"

"No, I loved her, but she wasn't my true mate. You might be," he said. His voice deeper than usual.

My heart stuttered and my pulse whooshed in my ears. I would have fallen over if I wasn't already leaning against the wall.

I beamed at the thought and was sure I looked goofy with my puppy-dog expression.

"I'd like that—" I finally said, and he kissed me before I finished my sentence.

Jason

I left Claire with Mel and entered Shawn's office.

"Just the wolf I needed to see," Shawn said without glancing up. "Tell me, what's happening with Claire. You two seem inseparable."

I closed the door and sat in a chair across from his desk. "I'd like to take a couple of days off. Hang with Claire until she shifts."

"You're serious about her?" He glanced up from his paperwork, his black hair falling into his intense blue eyes.

"I'd like to bond with her."

Shawn leaned back, his eyes widening, and sporting a smile I hadn't seen in a while. "I'm happy for you. Jeez, I'm jealous. I've been looking for my mate for three years and I think I never will." He shook his head. "I wanted to ask you to be my second."

"What happened to Killian?"

Shawn sighed. "He wants to start his own pack in the mountains." He nonchalantly waved his hand. "You know I'll hold none of my wolves back. But he couldn't have done it at a worst time."

"But things have calmed down, haven't they?"

"They have, but I've heard there's a bear motor-cycle gang going from town to town, causing trouble. I've just spoken with Sebastian, who received notice from the WAA. You know how it goes. One shifter hears something, and it filters down the line."

"But we have the WAA. You know they'll help."

"I know," he sighed again and louder. He seemed exhausted. "You handled things pretty well with Kevin and you're looking after Claire—"

"Did you want to take a couple of days off?"

He nodded. "There's a retreat for single alphas I want to attend. I'm worried by not having a mate, I'm weakening the pack. You know I can't have that. I'd much rather relinquish the pack to an alpha with a mate." He stared at me as if he was putting my name in the draw for that title.

"You know I don't want to lead. I'd gladly be your second and work with you, but I spend my time in the coffee shop and when Claire and I bond, I want pups soon after."

He smiled sadly. "Thank you, Jason. It means the world to have your support." He exhaled a shaky breath. "Okay, take as many days as you need with Claire. I'll stick around until you get back, and only attend the alpha retreat next month, you can manage things while I'm gone."

"Thanks, I can work with that. Tell me more about this retreat. I've never heard of it."

"It's run by a prestigious agency who matches alphas with potential mates. It doesn't work a hundred percent, but their stats are good." He handed me a sleek file with the company logo and inside neatly presented stats with graphs reflecting their success rate.

"A forty-eight percent success rate is actually good," I said as I leafed through the document. "It's impressive. Hopefully, they haven't manipulated the numbers."

"I know, but I'm not holding my breath. You know I've tried everything. Remember when I dated three women a night for a month, and I still didn't find anyone my beast wanted. After that month, it exhausted me from all the... you know what I mean. Since then, I just haven't bothered again."

I chuckled. Shawn was so grumpy he hadn't found his mate. Everybody stayed clear of him. He was a walking time bomb. "Yeah, I remember, and I do not want a repeat. Maybe this retreat will do you good. Maybe converse with the other alphas about that bear club."

"Hopefully they don't head this way."

I stood and shook his hand. "Whatever you need, alpha."

"Thanks, man."

"When is Killian leaving?"

"He already left."

I did not see that coming. It was abrupt, and he didn't say goodbye. "Why so suddenly?"

"He told me a few nights ago. With everything going on, there wasn't time to tell everyone. He was happy to leave by the back door. And I let him."

I didn't know if something serious had happened between them or if Killian had left willingly and silently. Whatever it was, I'd do what I could for Shawn. He wasn't a bad alpha, just... he was uptight and highly strung. Perhaps he needed this retreat more than anything else. The trip out of town would be good for him.

My thoughts crashed back to Claire, and I needed to get to my mate. "I gotta go check up on Claire."

"Call if you need anything." Shawn glanced down at his paperwork and got busy again. I shook my head. He needed to get away.

———

I found Claire and Mel giggling. When I entered the room, they fell silent. I didn't like that. Sometimes females knew how to get under my skin.

"What's going on?"

"Nothing, I'm done. Are you ready to leave?" Claire asked.

"Ready when you are, babe."

"Thanks Mel, and I'll let you know if there are any side effects."

"I've given Claire painkillers which might help, but you know those things don't work for us. But she can try them. And if anything strange happens, apart from her change, let me know and I'll come to you. I think my place is closer to your house than here anyway," Mel said, packing her medical bag.

"Thanks, Mel." Then I turned to Claire. "Are we going to my place?"

Claire beamed and nodded. Her smile reminded me of a naughty child's smile. Something was up.

'Hmm,' groaned Beast in my head. 'Make our female ours. Stop wasting time.'

'Yeah, I will.' I thought back to Beast and reached for Claire's hand. She slipped her smaller hand inside mine and rested her head against my shoulder. I loved it when she did that.

Claire

I had heard about the bonding ritual when I'd dated my ex-were-wolf and was glad we didn't go through with it. He was violently volatile and would've killed me if I didn't defend myself. And it relieved me he hadn't turned me back then.

When Jason left the room, Mel asked whether I was familiar with the bonding. I said I knew the gist of it; explaining there was an intense attraction one couldn't deny. Those mated had a sense of their chosen one. And no matter what they did, they couldn't deny the other.

Although I got to know Jason casually at first with our bantering at his coffee shop. I really got to know the man these last few days, and we'd grown extremely close. I knew I couldn't invalidate my feelings for him. My heart swelled with love each moment we spent together, and when we're apart, I longed for him. I felt like a love-sick fool.

"And you're aware that you'll share blood during your copulation?" Mel asked in a motherly tone.

"Good God, when last did I hear the word copulation. It's so formal, Mel," I snickered, causing her to laugh. "And to answer your question, I understand about the blood and spit swapping during sex." I enunciated the word 'sex' to see if Mel blushed, but she didn't she just laughed harder.

"Do you want to bond with him?"

"I do. I didn't experience love at first sight, but I'm warming up to the man. I can see us living an endless life together with many pups." The thought split my face in two.

Mel's eyes welled with unshed tears. "That would make our pack ecstatic. Fewer couples are having pups. And there are those who can't have. And you couldn't have chosen the nicest wolf to mate with. He really is a true protector."

The back of my throat ached when she said that. I really was lucky to have found him, or rather he had found me and didn't stop pursuing me until I finally said 'yes'.

He had done so much these last few days that I wanted to return the goodness. I wanted to spend the rest of my days making him as happy as he made me.

That once I was through the change, I'd want to start a family. And I hoped and prayed it worked out for us.

Mel hugged me, her grip firm and motherly. "And stay in that gorgeous house of his. And fill it up." She let go and patted my shoulder. "And you can scream as loud as you want. Nobody will call the cops on you," she said with a wicked wink.

I burst out laughing, and so did she, when Jason entered the medical room.

Claire

A nervousness swept through my entire body, leaving me chewing my fingernails. Jason noticed and pulled my fingers out of my mouth, bringing my hand to his, and kissed my knuckles.

"There's nothing to be nervous about."

"Ha! Easy for you to say. But thank you, I appreciate the support." I leaned against his shoulder as we traversed the pathway leading to his front door.

When we left the Wolf Pack, the medication Mel had given me started working. My stomach roiled, my skin crawled, and a fire raced through my veins. Everything felt like a contradiction, but it was Jason who grounded me. It was the dreaded feeling of losing control that left my nerves rattled.

Jason opened the front door, and I entered; his

house was warm, welcoming, and smelled of him. It had the bare necessities, but it looked like a man's house. It seriously needed a woman's touch.

"I know what you're thinking."

"Yeah, what's that?" I said with a smirk.

"You could do better with the place," he grinned, setting his keys on the kitchen island.

"Yep, I thought that. You've been alone for too long."

He approached with purpose. I suddenly felt like a deer caught in headlights. He cupped my face and bruised my lips.

He growled when he let go. "Beast wants to make you ours," he said, with his eyes still closed. When he opened them, they glowed yellow.

"Beast?"

He nodded. "My wolf. He chills in the metaphysical realm and has set his sights on you, babe. You don't have to answer now—"

"Yes!" I jumped into his arms, wrapped my legs around his waist, and kissed all over his face. "Tell Beast I said yes!"

Jason roared and ripped my clothing from my body. I let go of him and removed the tattered material.

"Jeez, I take it he approves?" I laughed.

"You're the only one for us."

"Enough talking, more kissing."

We embraced, wanting more of each other; more kissing, more touching, more everything. We found ourselves on the floor; but when I moaned, the carpet burning my shoulders, he picked me up again.

Jason pushed the coffee table back, giving us space, and threw a blanket on the carpet. He gently set me down on a blanket and proceeded to kiss down my body, nipping, teasing, and biting his way to the apex of my legs.

When I glanced down the line of my body, he'd left marks where he'd nibbled, marking his territory.

He caught me staring at him. "You're mine," he said, low and dirty, then licked my secret place that left me a quivering puddle.

"Ah," I moaned, and closed my eyes.

He teased my entrance with his tongue and inserted a finger. He growled as he coated his finger with my juices and pumped his finger inside me while his tongue tickled the spot that made my toes curl.

Jason continued his pleasant assault on my body while I writhed for him. When he inserted two fingers, my orgasm smashed into me with an intensity I'd never felt before. Not even the first time we made love.

My thoughts crashed into each other as I thought about him, the growing love I felt for him, and having his pups. And him making me his.

My eyes shot open when he removed his fingers.

"Don't worry, there's more to come… literally," he grinned.

I reached for Jason as he hovered above me like he was about to do a pushup when I recoiled. Something felt strange. An icy shiver ran down my back. My vision blurred at the sides and then tunneled.

I opened my eyes, staring at the floor and on my hands and knees. Sucking in deep breaths of air as I tried to steady my racing heart.

"You're okay," Jason consoled me, rubbing my back. "Stop fighting the change, Claire. Give in," he whispered near the shell of my ear, sounding dream-like and mysterious.

It felt like I was giving birth, and it sounded like it. Sweat dripped to the floor, my hands bunched into fists, and pain shot down my spine.

"Allow your wolf to take over, Claire. Stop fighting her. Let her out." His voice echoed inside my head.

"I'm trying, dammit," I screamed as more pain burst through my head. It felt like my eyes were about to pop out of their sockets. My back arched, and I shrieked.

Sucking in another deep breath, I closed my eyes and exhaled slowly. Piercing yellow eyes stared back at me through my mind. It felt as though someone had shone a light directly into each closed eye.

Her face came into view, and she was breathtakingly beautiful. My white wolf.

I choked on a sob, realizing I'd match Jason's white wolf, and that I wasn't that ghastly color of the wolf who had bitten me.

Her face neared, and she licked my cheek, relaxing me. I welcomed her inside; I needed her to do her thing. And I gave myself over to her.

My wolf howled, and another wolf howled with her. In that second, she ran toward me, through me, inside me. She burst through my body; twisting my limbs, snapping my joints, and changing my body.

I awoke to another wolf staring at me; Jason. He scent marked me and licked near my mouth—a kiss. He howled, and I joined him.

The feeling of being inside a wolf, of being my wolf, was liberating. I walked on my paws like it was the most natural thing ever. After walking on two legs my whole life, it surprised me I didn't trip and fall.

'You're a natural,' Jason whispered inside my head.

'How can I hear you?'

'We're fated mates, Claire. I am yours; you are mine.'

'I love you.'

'I love you, too,' Jason's voice echoed in my mind as his much larger wolf licked my face, kissing me. *'Do you want to go running?'*

'Yes!'

We darted out the back door toward his backyard, that opened to the forest and beyond. I followed him through brushes, over broken tree stumps, and over rocks until we came to a stream.

I stood beside him and stared at my reflection in the water. His white wolf was magnificent. Mine was just as white, but my ears were gray.

'You're beautiful, my she-wolf.'

I laughed—in my head—'cause there was no way to laugh with a muzzle like mine. I rested my gigantic head against his. My change complete; content in my new form.

'I don't need the moon to change?' I asked once I could think properly again.

'No, it's rare, but it does happen.'

'Does that mean anything?'

'Only that you are powerful enough to shift whenever you want to. And the moon doesn't pull your beast through you. It's a rare gift.'

That made me think about the ranks within the Wolf Pack. *'If I'm as powerful as you say, will you train me? Then I can join the ranks.'*

'I'd love nothing more. But—'

'Pups?'

'Yes, I want us to have pups as soon as we can.'

'We can start now.' I said and started running back toward his house.

I darted out of his grasp, into his house, and jumped onto his couch.

'How do I change back?'

'Command it, and your wolf will return to the meta-physical realm.'

I didn't know how to *'command it'* but I asked her nicely to retreat and to give me back my body. My change back into my human form was smoother and not as hurtful.

I flexed my muscles and stretched my naked body on the couch. I wanted to curl up in a ball and sleep until movement caught my eye.

Jason laid on his side, staring at me like an apex predator. I returned the glare and climbed off the couch like a cat and stalked my man on the floor. I pushed him onto his back and planted delicate kisses against his skin. A low rumbling growl came from the base of his throat when I reached for his erection.

"How do you feel?" he asked with his eyes closed.

"I feel good. Better than good, I feel great. Now shush, I'm taking what's mine." I covered him with my mouth and stroked up and down.

Moans escaped his mouth, and his right hand grabbed my ass. I was kneeling as I pleasured him. The moment I lifted my ass slightly, Jason's fingers found my delicate folds, and he moaned louder. He sat up; I yelped when he grabbed me and settled me on his lap.

"I can't wait to sink inside you."

He reached for his cock and rubbed against me. Slowly I sank down onto him and he filled me, stretching me. I moved up and down his steel length, enjoying the feel of him as our bodies melded together.

"I love you," I said.

Jason grabbed my waist, flipped me onto my back and thrusted deeply. "Be mine?" he asked, his eyes glowing yellow and his fangs elongated.

The thought of sinking my teeth into him and tasting his blood made my fangs lengthen. And I nodded.

Jason smiled, hovered above me as he kept his sweet rhythm. I felt the pinch of his sharp teeth pierce my skin, followed by him drinking.

A deep desire to make him mine enveloped me. Without thinking, I pulled him closer and bit into his shoulder.

The moment his sweet blood touched my lips, my world shattered as our heart beats joined, our souls entwined, as our bodies became one.

I drank from him as he drank from me, and I couldn't be happier.

Our bond sealed and blossomed like a flower, and

I felt his happiness shine through me like a new dawn.

I heard whispers of his thoughts, and they were of love and happiness. I projected my love for him and felt him receive it with pride.

He stopped drinking, as did I, and came into my view. At first his features were blurry then when the stars dissipated, I grinned at his winsome smile.

We kissed with each other's blood still in our mouths, and our bond solidified as our orgasms smashed into us at the same time.

I spasmed around him as he released his heated seed within me.

The ground shifted as power coursed through us; a power so great that it could heal a village. My skin tightened, my eyes brightened, as the power flowed through us, in our veins, and through the earth.

The magnitude of the power we unleashed was not lost on us. I felt his thoughts as if they were my own.

"Together we are greater," I said without thinking, not knowing where the words came from.

Jason nodded. "Shawn said a mated alpha's power becomes substantial once the bond is complete, but I didn't know it would be like this." He bruised my lips once more. "I love you."

We held each other until the sun came up the next morning.

It was a new day, a new life, and new beginnings.

I'd met a man I thought I didn't want, yet I needed him more than I wanted to admit.

I'd long forgotten about my ex-were-wolf and Erik. They were blips on a radar I no longer needed.

Jason was my beginning, and my new everything.

He pulled me into the curve of his body and kissed the nape of my neck.

"I never wanted to say anything about your scars before because I knew it hurt for you to speak about your past." Jason kissed my temple. "But I'm happy to report that our bonding has healed those pesky marks."

"What?" I said, sounding flabbergasted, and glanced down at my naked chest. The deep scars caused by claws no longer ruined my skin. The burn marks on my back from cigarettes now gone. And the scar from a sharp blade on my right breast had disappeared. "That… that's amazing. I don't understand what it means." I gasped, turning around, and faced Jason. "But it isn't the marks. You would've loved me with them, anyway."

He nodded. "I love you, the person," — he pointed at my chest, — "your body is just a bonus," he teased, wiggling his eyebrows. Then he said in a serious tone. "I mean it. We're bound forever, Claire. You've made me the happiest wolf alive. Awoo." He howled.

I joined him in a howl, then we laughed.

I settled against him again, my finger trailing the scars no longer there.

For an orphan who was first neglected, then abused, I'd finally found my home with a man who was now my everything.

———

The next day, I moved in with Jason. My one-bedroom apartment hardly had any furniture, but we managed to fit everything in his much larger house.

Mel had taken another blood sample after my transfusion and was happy to report I was were-rabies free. The last thing we needed was a deterrent to stop us from having pups.

I had the usual female check-up, and my OB/GYN gave me his blessing. He saw no reason not to have babies. I didn't tell him I'd be having human pups. That was a conversation for another day.

Blaire shrieked into the phone when I told her about my bonding. I went deaf in that ear for a few seconds. She said I could work anywhere I wanted to. But if Jason wanted me barefoot and pregnant in front of the stove, I could do that too. I told her I would continue working for her for a long time. I enjoyed what they did. And one day I'd like to join them on cases, but only after I had pups.

One good thing about living with Jason, I now had all the free coffee I could stomach; not forgetting those yummy chocolate muffins.

Life was good.

Jason, a dream come true.

And I his forever mate.

Nothing could go wrong.

Special Mentions

Thank you to my readers, old and new, for taking a chance on my books.

You are the reason I write the stories I do. As long as you keep reading, I'll keep writing.

I'm truly humbled by your support and encouragement.

A special shout out to **Tammy at Book Nook Nuts** for helping me find the gremlins.

From Me

Dear Reader

I write in as many genres as I love reading in. There are so many stories swarming inside my head that I could never just choose one.

Horrors are my guilty pleasures. I love writing short stories filled with dark humor and the occult with a twist ending.

Urban fantasy and Paranormal Romance are where I love to spend my time and I have so many books planned that I don't have enough time (*but I'll get there*).

And lastly, my **thrillers**. Who doesn't love sitting on the edge of their seat while reading about what goes on inside the antagonists mind. Well, I love writing about them.

You can view all my books on my website. They come in ebook format as well as paperback, and most are in hard cover.

Come find me at the usual hangouts, say *hi*, and tell me about yourself.

Until the next book, stay safe and keep reading.

To get **FREE** stories please visit my page at:
https://www.ngraybooks.com

facebook.com/ngraybooks

twitter.com/NGrayBooks

instagram.com/ngraybooks

bookbub.com/profile/n-gray

patreon.com/ngraybooks

tiktok.com/@ngrayauthor

Thanks for Reading

If you enjoyed this book, please consider **leaving a review** at the site where you purchased it from? A one or two line would be fantastic. Each review helps authors like me reach new readers.

Thank you!

Also by

Please be advised!

I write in FOUR genres, hopefully one of them tickles your fancy...

Short Story Collections

What's for Dinner?

The Hunter

The Package (Make Them Pay Anthology)

Book of the Dead

Horror Features Series

Creature Features

Monster Features

Dana Mulder Thriller Series

Nightcrawler

Deadly Pattern

Devil Mountain

Chasing Evil

Dana Mulder Omnibus

Stand-alone Thriller

Lady Killer

Blaire Thorne Urban Fantasy Series

Ulysses Exposed

Voodoo Priest

Butterflies & Hurricanes

Salvation

Blaire Thorne Omnibus

Underworld Legacy

**Shifter Days, Vampire Nights, & Demons in between
Series**

Dark Tarot

Wolf Retreat

Lady Hawk and her Mountain Man

The Fixer

Twisted

Night Hunter

Kai

Hidden Shifter

Wolf